Crosswise

"The suspense starts on the first page and doesn't let up. A unique setting with unforgettable characters."
—Terrence McCauley, author
of *Sympathy for the Devil*

"Briskly paced and precise as a Sunday crossword, this mystery hooks you fast, reels you in, and keeps you dangling in suspense till the very last page."
—Scott Adlerberg, author of
Jungle Horses and *Graveyard Love*

"Stands as a glorious bastard child of *Goodfellas* and *The Golden Girls*...further cements S.W. Lauden as one of the best new voices in mystery and crime."
—Angel Luis Colón, author of
The Fury of Blacky Jaguar

"A taut, suspenseful romp through the Redneck Riviera with an entertaining cast of characters"
—Michael Lister, author of *Innocent Blood*

"Femme fatale, Florida heat, and clues tougher to figure out than a *NY Times* Sunday crossword puzzle. Sunsplashed noir with New York City attitude. A fun read that will keep you guessing until the end."
—Matt Coyle, author of the Anthony Award
winning Rick Cahill crime series

"S.W. Lauden marches into Carl Hiassen's Florida to mark his territory with whip-crack dialogue, tight plotting, and hellfire pacing all of which will leave you gasping for breath."
—Eryk Pruitt, author of *Dirtbags* and *Hashtag*

CROSSED
BONES

Erica,
Crime fiction
is going to the
DOGS!

OTHER BOOKS BY S.W. LAUDEN

Tommy & Shayna Crime Capers
Crosswise
Crossed Bones

Greg Salem Mysteries
Bad Citizen Corporation
Grizzly Season
Hang Time (*)

(*) - forthcoming

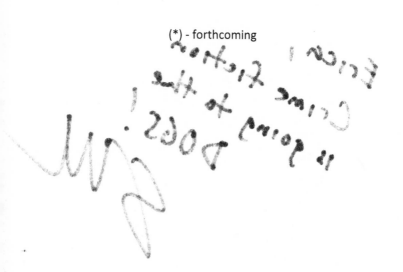

S. W. LAUDEN

CROSSED BONES

DOWN & OUT
BOOKS

Down & Out Books
3959 Van Dyke Rd, Ste. 265
Lutz, FL 33558
www.DownAndOutBooks.com

The characters and events in this book are fictitious. Any similarity to real persons, living or dead, is coincidental and not intended by the author.

Cover design by J.T. Lindroos

ISBN: 1-943402-57-4
ISBN-13: 978-1-943402-57-1

For Spin Echo

ADRIFT

It was a rundown, two-story clapboard house several miles off the guidebook maps. Empty kegs were stacked three-high on either side of the screen door like dented tin soldiers. A mangy dog slept on a shabby couch under the cracked window out front. It definitely wasn't the kind of place tourists would ever visit—unless they were lost or unlucky. Shayna Billups was feeling a little of both these days.

She threw her red convertible into park and pushed the car door open, swinging her long legs out into the street. It felt good to stand up after so many hours on the road. She stretched and yawned, shifting the hem of her tight skirt back down with a practiced wiggle.

The cracked wooden porch wobbled under her high heels, like an uneven pile of firewood. Zydeco music wafted out of the bar to greet her, along with the smell of fried shrimp and stale beer. The Keel Hall might pass for quaint if it didn't look like it was about to collapse. She was reaching for the door when somebody racked the slide on a shotgun behind her.

"I wouldn't go in there if I was you."

His voice was slow and deep. Shayna brought her hands up, calmly turning around.

He had menacing eyes and spiky blond hair that glistened in the afternoon sun. His tattooed arms were bursting from the sleeves of his too-tight T-shirt. It took Shayna a beat to realize that there were also two women, one on either side of him. They both wore too much make-up and ear-to-ear smiles. It was obvious to Shayna that running a bar in New Orleans had taken a nasty toll on her high school friends.

The man brought his gun down, flashing a mischievous grin.

"These two put me up to it, I swear."

Shayna lowered her hands, bringing one to rest on a strategically cocked hip.

"I almost had a heart attack, you asshole."

His eyes traced her curves, from her high heels to her pouting lips. He looked like a rescue dog setting eyes on its first steak.

"You passing through or planning to stay a while, sugar?"

"Well," Shayna said, twisting her blonde hair with an index finger. "That all depends…"

The man took a step forward, as if in a trance. The woman standing on his left smacked him hard across the head, snapping him out of it. He spun around to give her a piece of his mind and caught an open hand across the cheek.

He gave Shayna one more glance and wandered around the side of the building shaking his head, the shotgun on his shoulder. The two women rushed up onto the porch. Georgia had been the head cheerleader back in high school, but looked more like a linebacker now. She was tall and thick, with broad shoulders and wide hips. Her greasy, yellow hair was the color of stale French fries. She threw an arm around Shayna, squeezing the air right out of her.

Ida was a fireplug by comparison. She was short and stocky, with limp brown curls framing a pock-marked face. It didn't look to Shayna like either of them went very long between drinks or meals.

Ida gave Shayna's ass a firm squeeze.

"Damn, girl. I see you packed your trunk."

"Thanks. I had a little work done last year."

Ida glanced up at Shayna's chest, screwing her lips into a smirk.

"And that ain't all. What brings you down to the Big Easy?"

Shayna chose her words carefully. She'd found

out a little too late that killing your husband doesn't pay, at least not right away. The bitchy lady handling the insurance claim told her a payout could take up to a month. That left Shayna without anywhere to be.

"Heading to Los Angeles eventually, but there's no big rush. Thought I'd stop by here to see what kind of trouble the three of us could get into."

Georgia and Ida exchanged a look that told Shayna she had them on the hook. She had to be patient while reeling them in.

"I hope I'm not imposing. You two must have your hands full running a fine establishment like this."

Shayna motioned to a faded sign by the front door. It swung in a slight breeze that delivered the muddy smell of the Mississippi River mingled with the scent of olive trees and piss. The Keel Hall's website made it sound like a swanky Las Vegas re-sort, but it was nothing more than a pirate-themed dive bar that the locals called Keely's.

Georgia stepped forward with a broad smile on her frying pan face.

"Glad you like it. We're actually looking for a new bartender, if you feel like staying a while."

"You'll make a killing in tips," Ida quickly added. "We'll even throw in room and board."

Shayna felt conflicted, despite the fact that everything was going exactly like she wanted it to. She didn't regret killing her husband, but really missed planning it. All of the plotting and scheming, the complicated lies and manipulations, had given her a sense of purpose that felt like a missing limb these days. She hadn't just gotten revenge on that abusive, pill-popping son-of-a-bitch; she'd fooled everybody in Seatown, Florida—*my hometown*—including the police. And now all of that hard work was reduced to a check she was waiting to get in the mail.

The whole thing had been about the cash, but now it didn't seem like it was enough. She craved a new adventure, something to lose herself in completely. Unfortunately, the person she most wanted to share it with was back in Seatown. And he probably hated her for everything she'd put him through.

I've already ruined Tommy Ruzzo's life twice before, she thought. *A third time might finally kill him.*

Shayna shook her head, chasing those thoughts away. She needed a stiff drink, and maybe something a little stiffer than that. Anything to obliterate the unwanted memories she was trying to outrun.

"Aren't you two sweet? Buy me a drink and I'll think it over."

"Hell, yeah," Georgia said. "We should get you inside before the neighborhood dogs come sniffing around anyway."

Shayna waved the compliment away with the flick of her wrist.

"Speaking of dogs. Who was your friend with the gun? He's cute, in a scummy sort of way."

Ida dug her press-on nails into Shayna's arm until she almost drew blood. Her voice was a smoky growl.

"That's our bouncer, Adam, but keep your paws off of him—he's mine, all mine."

Shayna made a mental note to avoid the bouncer while she was there. She wasn't afraid of Ida, but she definitely didn't need another murder on her hands. *At least not right away.*

Georgia made a sweeping gesture with her arm as they entered. The interior was even more run down than the outside, but the soft blue lights gave it a pleasant underwater glow. The two large fish tanks behind the short wooden bar looked like they hadn't been cleaned in months. A faded Jolly Roger hung from the ceiling overhead, dancing like a ghost in the breeze of a circular fan. Anchors and helms adorned the walls at odd intervals, mostly to cover up water stains. In between were thrift store paintings with vaguely nautical themes, mixed in with framed pirate maps of every shape and size.

A few of the scattered tables were full, but almost nobody spoke. Ida jumped behind the bar to grab a shaker. Georgia and Shayna climbed up onto stools near a stooped, older man. He wore a black stocking cap and had a thick white beard that hung down to his prominent potbelly. A half empty beer mug sat still on the bar in front of him, as forgotten and lonely-looking as its owner. All he needed was an eyepatch or a pegleg and he could be the center-piece of the bar's worn-out decor.

Shayna couldn't take her eyes off of him. She leaned over to whisper in Georgia's ear.

"Please tell me he's an actor that you hire to sit there."

Georgia snuck a peek around her.

"Lafitte? Hell, he used to own this place."

Ida set two coconut-shaped mugs in front of them. Shayna watched thick foam bubble over the lip of hers, oozing like spit down to her wrinkled cocktail napkin. A green toothpick floated on top, buoyed by a dried out wedge of pineapple and a shriveled maraschino cherry.

"What the hell kind of drink is that?"

Georgia hoisted hers up in a toast.

"The kind that gets you drunk."

Shayna finished hers off in a couple of gulps. The sugary rum burned going down, but left her feeling warm all over. She licked the foam from her upper lip, slamming the empty coconut to the bar.

"What's a woman have to do to get laid around here?"

AND A BOTTLE OF RUM

Tommy Ruzzo was soaking wet. The Florida rain still took him by surprise, especially when he was drunk. That was most of the time these days, and working as a bouncer at The Rusty Pelican didn't help. Mikey couldn't pay much, but he let Ruzzo live on his fishing boat for free. And Ruzzo always had an open tab at the bar—a perk that he took full advantage of, even on his days off.

He pushed through the front door, shaking his head like a dog. Water flung from his thick black hair, dotting a couple of nearby tables and chairs. They were worn and empty, like the rest of the place. Monday used to be "Comedy Open Mic Night," but Mikey canceled it after his old friend, Jesse Lee Cavanaugh, went on a killing spree that almost cost Ruzzo his life.

"3 AM" by Matchbox Twenty blared from the jukebox as Ruzzo climbed up onto his usual stool. He knew better than to complain about Mikey's terrible taste in music, so he focused on the volume instead.

"Does it have to be so freakin' loud?"

"What? Oh…"

Mikey lifted a remote, bringing the volume down from intolerable to merely deafening. His long hair was cropped short now, and spiky on top. It made his bloated red face look like a giant puffer fish.

"New usual?"

Ruzzo nodded. He used to be a whisky man, but these days he drank rum. It went well with his baggy Hawaiian shirt, khaki shorts and flip-flops. His compact frame had gotten paunchy around the middle, and his cheeks and chin were more rounded. He'd come to town a rock-hard New Yorker, but now he was soft like the white sand beaches that lined the Gulf Coast. His surrender to Florida was complete. *There are worse places to die.*

It didn't help that Ruzzo was broke and out of options. Mikey set two shot glasses down, filling them to the lip with Bacardi 151. He lifted one up in a shaky toast.

"Here's to swimmin' behind bow-legged women."

Ruzzo froze, the drink midway between his lips and the bar.

"What the hell kind of pervert toast is that?"

"No idea. Something my dad used to say."

"Sounds like dumbass runs in your family."

Mikey clenched his teeth into a smile, but let it go. They each knocked their drinks back in a single gulp. Mikey immediately filled their glasses again.

"Any news from Sgt. Badeaux about Jesse Lee?"

Ruzzo tensed. His free hand travelled down to the scar on his gut. The doctors said it was a miracle that the bullet only grazed him. The jury was still out as far as he was concerned.

"Sgt. Badeaux's a rat bastard. Let's talk about something else for a change."

Mikey's eyes shifted to the front window. A line of cars crawled along the highway out front. The grey skies overhead pulsated with the flash of distant lightning.

"Looks like the storm's moving on."

Ruzzo grunted in response. Mikey picked a towel up and started polishing a murky pint glass.

"Any word from Shayna?"

Ruzzo finished off his second shot, slamming the glass down on the bar. It hit the wood with a loud crack.

"You're killing me!"

"Sorry. There ain't much happening in Seatown these days."

Ruzzo's shoulders slumped.

"No shit. I'll drink to that."

Mikey topped his shot off again.

"That's what I like about you, Ruzzo. You'll drink to just about anything."

TREASURE MAP

Shayna stood behind the bar at Keely's three weeks later. Her hands shook uncontrollably thanks to a sustained drunken blackout. From what she could piece together, she, Ida and Georgia had been living on a steady diet of beignets, rum and cocaine.

Blurry memories sailed across her psyche like ghost ships. Maybe they'd worn beads and danced on tables, shot pool and skinny-dipped in the Mississippi River. Or maybe they hadn't. There might have been fireworks at some point, or was it gunshots? Whatever the truth was, it seemed like exactly the kind of debaucherous escape that she had always enjoyed—until things fell apart. *Why do things always fall apart?*

Some memories were clearer than others. Her skin crawled when she remembered how Georgia and Ida dragged her from bar to bar like a prize cow, telling everybody that she was their "hot new piece of ass." Shayna played along; happily slurping down free drinks while every lecherous boozehound in town hit on her. Her new bosses loved all the free promotion for Keely's, but got more and more jealous as the week wore on. Shayna barely noticed until their scowls and insults turned violent.

The flashbacks got worse as the hours dragged on. She caught glimpses of eager men in strange beds, topless carriage rides, and an endless line of blow that extended the length of Bourbon Street. She imagined herself crawling along the cobblestones with a straw in her nose, her heart almost beating through her chest. *But at least I'm not thinking about Tommy Ruzzo.*

And then, just like that, she was thinking about him. Again.

Shayna was desperate for someone to talk to. Anybody who could help her escape the dark thoughts that crept into her mind the minute she was sober and alone. A little hair of the dog might do the trick, but the thought of alcohol made her want to puke. She was seriously starting to question her hard and fast rule about never buying cocaine for personal use.

She searched the bar in desperation, but Lafitte was the only customer there. He'd been nursing the same flat beer for an hour, staring off into space. Shayna wandered over to the small sink directly under the bar in front of him. Nothing got her two best assets jiggling quite like the automatic glass washers submerged there.

Lafitte's bloodshot eyes shifted downward, but his expression didn't change.

"Nice knockers."

His voice was soft and gravelly, as if he'd recently swallowed broken glass. Shayna tittered like a schoolgirl in response, but kept cleaning glasses. She had him right where she wanted him.

"The rest of you still work as well as your eyes, old man?"

"Not really, but at least all of my parts are real. Those things hurt when they sewed them on?"

He nodded at her chest and winked. She did a terrible job of acting offended by his question.

"What makes you think they're fake?"

"Nothing in nature moves like that, sweetheart."

He lifted his beer to take sip. She grabbed a towel, wiping the bar beneath it.

"Ready for another?"

Lafitte studied the mug in his hand, as if discovering it was there. His nod was almost imperceptible when he set it back down. Shayna pulled the tap to draw him a fresh draft. The golden liquid caught the soft light as she slid it his way.

"This one's on me."

"As long as you're feeling generous, can you give me a light?"

He produced a bent cigarette from his shirt pocket. Shayna set a glass ashtray down in front of him. The image of a gold doubloon on the bottom was smudged black from use and abuse. She pulled out a Keely's matchbook, quickly producing a flame. He took a long drag, smoke escaping from his nostrils without any obvious effort.

"You remind me of my daughter."

Shayna's shoulders relaxed a little now that she had something else to focus on.

"Really? What's her name?"

"No idea. I just made her up. Seemed like you were looking for somebody to tell you a fairy tale."

"Well, that's messed up."

"You wouldn't want to hear any stories about my family, anyway. Trust me."

Shayna tried to act mad, but knew she had no right. That didn't mean she was willing to let him off the hook. He owed her now.

"Then tell me about this dump. What's with all the pirate crap?"

The cigarette danced on his lip as he laughed. He sounded like a stuttering bullfrog with emphysema.

"You want to hear a really crazy story? Go grab that map off the wall over there."

Lafitte spun around on his stool, raising his arm like a slow-moving compass. She was up on her tippy toes, trying to see where his finger would eventually land. It stopped on a large, boxy frame near the men's room door.

What the hell, she thought. *My shift's almost over anyway.*

Shayna stepped from behind the bar and went to grab the strange artifact. She nearly ran straight into Ida walking across the room. Her boss didn't seem happy to see her.

"Why aren't you working?"

Shayna motioned to the empty room, but Ida's angry expression didn't change. Georgia emerged from the women's bathroom right then, shaking water off of her hands. She took one look at Shayna and sneered.

"Fill up the paper towels in there before you clock out."

Shayna watched them walk away together. She waited until they were behind the bar before she went over to the old frame, pulling it from the wall. Something rattled as she walked. She studied the small piece of parchment trapped inside when she set it down in front of Lafitte. It was about the size and shape of a jagged saw blade with faded black markings spread across it. His eyes danced from her face to the map.

"Know anything about pirates?"

"Only what I've seen in movies."

Lafitte rolled his eyes.

"This map belonged to a bona fide pirate, not some Hollywood wannabe. His name was Captain Edward Aurora."

"Never heard of him."

"Hardly anybody has, outside of North Carolina. You know about Blackbeard?"

"Of course."

"Captain Aurora was a lot bigger, and twice as mean. He and a few other English sailors got shipwrecked on a Caribbean island when he was about eighteen. It took the Royal Navy a couple of years to find them, but he was the only one still alive when they did. His front teeth were filed into sharp points by then, and his blond beard was stained red with blood. They say he'd developed a taste for human flesh."

"Holy shit. That's amazing."

"I know, and this was before Novocain. He joined a pirate crew a few months after he got back, and became captain during a bloody mutiny. They say he captured fifteen ships before he hanged for treason three years later. This map supposedly leads to his buried treasure."

"Really? Where?"

"Somewhere on Corcoran Island, in the Outer Banks of North Carolina."

They sat at the bar together for the next couple of hours. He spun the whole incredible tale while she eagerly nodded along. He said that small piece of parchment was part of a much bigger map, pointing out that it was the most important piece because of that letter X in the center.

"Look closely. It's a tiny skull with crossed bones. Somebody finds the rest of that map and they'll find the treasure."

"Where's the other half?"

"I'd start by looking in Stonehaven, if I was a younger man."

His finger was still planted firmly on the map when Shayna finally looked up. She was surprised to see that Keely's was filling up with a rowdy crowd. Georgia and Ida both looked like they were sleepwalking as they filled orders and drank themselves awake. Neither of them made eye contact with Shayna.

She turned back to speak with Lafitte, but he was already across the room hanging the map back on the wall. The bouncer was sitting on his stool instead. He looked her up and down, practically licking his lips.

"Hey, Shayna. I've got something for you."

She craned her neck to look for the old man, but he was nowhere to be seen.

"Seat's taken, Adam."

"Was Lafitte telling you his pirate stories?"

"Be nice, asshole. He's sweet."

"Hey, now. You're sexy when you're mean."

The bouncer reached into his leather jacket, producing an official-looking envelope. Part of Shayna wished it was another map, until she saw it was addressed to her. She reached for it, but he pulled it back at the last second.

"I thought that might get your attention, but I've got something even better."

He reached into his other pocket, pulling out a tightly folded piece of paper. It was about the size of a matchbook and practically bursting with cocaine. She watched for a moment as he flipped it between his fingers like a magician would a coin—before fumbling it to the floor.

The bouncer leapt from his chair to recover the coke. Shayna took the opportunity to snatch the envelope from his outstretched hand. She spun on her barstool and sliced it open with her fingernail. The life insurance check inside was made out to her in the amount of three hundred thousand dollars.

She felt the bouncer's hot breath on the back of her neck. He leaned in to put his arm around her shoulder.

"Damn, girl! You hit the lottery. Let's celebrate."

He waved the bindle under her nose. She tried to ignore him, but there was no doubt he'd gotten her attention.

Shayna looked over to where Georgia and Ida were mixing up cocktails and flirting with the pathetic regulars. She could clearly picture them doing the same thing, night after night, for the next twenty years. Then she imagined herself right there beside them, weathered, wrinkled and washed out. The thought of it made her skin crawl.

That's when she made up her mind. It was definitely time to leave New Orleans, but not without a little going away party for two. Shayna grabbed the bouncer's wrist and led him upstairs.

Her dreams teemed with pirates that night. She imagined wooden boats filled with swashbuckling men who swung from ropes with swords in their teeth. Buried treasure chests dotted the white sandy beaches of a thousand tiny islands, where palm trees swayed in the violent tropical breezes. Powder flashed from the flared muzzle of a blunderbuss as she wandered through the bloody battle in her tattered wench's dress. Cannons erupted all around her, spitting out fire and filling the air with acrid smoke.

Smoke.

Shayna's eyes shot open. The bouncer was passed out cold in the bed beside her. Strange voices were screaming downstairs. It felt too late for the bar to be open, but she was too disoriented to know for sure. The familiar scent of burning wood filled her nostrils. She tiptoed over to the bedroom door, cracking it open an inch or two.

A policeman was frantically waving his flashlight at the top of the stairs. The yellow beam danced across the tendrils of gray smoke that curled around his boots. He was yelling for everybody to get out of the building before it burned to the ground. She slammed the door shut, gathering her scattered clothes from the floor. It's nearly impossible to put a thong on backwards, but Shayna almost managed to do so in her rush to get dressed.

She tossed the rest of her possessions into a bag and went over to the bed. Two chalky white lines were still laid out on the nightstand. She grabbed a rolled up dollar bill and polished them off. The bouncer's pistol was there too, along with his keys and wallet. She fished a couple of hundred-dollar bills out, tucking them into her bra. She definitely didn't need the money now, but that didn't stop her from taking it.

She reached down, pinching his nostrils shut. It seemed like an eternity before he sprang up in a panic.

"What the hell's going on?"

"There's some kind of fire. Cops are all over place."

He rubbed his eyes and jumped out of bed.

"This has Ida written all over it."

Shayna opened the door, heading downstairs without looking back. Shadows dashed through the orange glow in the barroom. She hung a right at the bottom, hugging the wall until she reached the men's bathroom. The boxy frame was still hanging right where Lafitte had left it. She pulled it from the hook, shoving it into her bag.

Fire trucks wailed down the street outside. Georgia and Ida were seated on the curb when Shayna finally emerged. Several policemen hovered around them, barking orders into their radios. The women's faces twisted into horrible, forced smiles when they caught sight of her.

Georgia waved her over. Ida leaned forward

when Shayna walked up; her voice was a scratchy hiss.

"See what you get when you sleep with my man?"

It was all too familiar for Shayna. She needed to get out of there before the panic took over. There was no way she could be associated with another fire without somebody putting two and two to-gether. Shayna might not have started this one with a match, but they could still trace the spark back to her.

She slipped by, making a beeline for her red convertible. It was parked across the street and down the block—far enough away from the commotion that it wouldn't be blocked in by any emergency vehicles. She climbed behind the wheel, started the engine and stomped on the gas. There was nowhere for her to go, no place she had to be. Her head spun with the lonely possibilities, but the tank was full enough to get her out of town.

She looked down at her bag in the passenger seat. A corner of the frame was poking out like a tiny wooden arrow. She reached over and snatched it up, Lafitte's final words running through her mind.

I'd start by looking in Stonehaven...

Shayna took the first on-ramp. She didn't slow

down until she crossed the North Carolina state line thirteen hours later. From there she only had to follow the road signs leading the way to "The Home of Captain Aurora."

ONE YEAR LATER

THE SCOURGE OF STONEHAVEN

Shayna sucked the last of her fruity rum drink through a straw. She set the glass down on the edge of the bathtub and sighed. Flickering candlelight filled the steamy bathroom with golden, swirling ghosts that danced all around her. They were nothing compared to the ones that haunted her thoughts.

She'd been a business owner in North Carolina for almost a year, but still wondered how Tommy Ruzzo was doing back in Seatown—or if he was even there still. It was hard to believe that he would stay in Florida very long without her, or maybe that was wishful thinking. She knew in her heart that he belonged in New York, but wasn't sure he could go back after she'd so completely destroyed his world.

She lifted a leg, pressing her foot against the cold tiles surrounding the tub. Looking back, it was clear that her problems started the minute she rolled into Stonehaven. Shayna figured out right away that the entire town was cuckoo for Captain

Aurora. Only half the residents claimed to be related to the legendary pirate, but every one of them dressed up like him at least once a year. She immediately put her mind to figuring out how she could use their obsession to her advantage.

She slid down in the tub until her head was completely submerged; her blonde hair was a golden helmet when she broke the surface a moment later. A light ocean breeze blew in through the open window as she stood up to step from the tub. She lifted her arms in the air, goosebumps covering her naked body.

Two bearded men swooped in from the darkened corners of the room. Their white linen shirts billowed like sails as they approached. The swords on their leather belts clanged and swung. They both wore large hoop earrings and three-cornered hats. Her perfect new breasts barely moved as the two pirates gently toweled her off.

"Did you guys enjoy the show?"

The one on her left nodded eagerly. His real name was Kevin, but he went by Edward in honor of Captain Aurora. Shayna thought he was a little short for the role, but what he lacked in height he more than made up for with intensity. He'd trained to be a pilot in the Air Force before drinking his way to a less-then-honorable discharge.

Edward was the first of many pirates Shayna collected from the streets, and the one who shared her bed. His wiry frame and hypnotic gaze were a dangerous combination that she used to her advantage at every opportunity. It didn't hurt that he kind of resembled Tommy Ruzzo.

He was yet another Captain Aurora impersonator when they met, posing with tourists for five bucks a shot. But there was something different about him, a certain quality that made him stand out in that snarling crowd. It could have been his high school theater training, or it might have simply been his good looks. Whatever the reason, his thick, braided beard and passable English accent made him a star in Shayna's eyes. She got her first wench outfit soon after meeting him and became his manager.

Edward had been a great partner ever since, but she knew not to trust him completely. Shayna gave him a wink as he ran the towel down the length of her spine. The corners of his mouth turned up in a crooked smile while she barked out more orders.

"Make sure you don't miss...a single...spot..."

The pirate on her right growled, "Of course, m'lady." She had no idea what his name was, and didn't really care. But she did like the feel of his strong hands on her thighs.

"Finish up and leave Edward and me alone."

The pirate did as he was told, closing the door behind him. Shayna reached down and gave Edward a playful squeeze.

"Why don't you join me in the bedroom before we go plundering later tonight?"

He never said no. Shayna liked to think it was because of her perfectly sculpted body, but she knew that jealousy played a part too. If Edward wasn't up for the job, there were seven more out in the living room ready to take his place. *Or maybe they're back out on the streets of Stonehaven dealing coke for me.*

She never could keep track, but all eight of them kept coming back night after night. It could have been the free drugs, but Shayna liked to think it was something else. That this was her private pirate army and—best of all—nobody in the city had any idea they were being invaded. *Well, almost nobody.*

There was one person in town that kept a close eye on Shayna. She assumed he was another dirty old man when they first met at a bar on the waterfront. He introduced himself as Charles that night and offered to buy her a cocktail while drinking her in with his eyes. It wasn't until a couple of his biker bodyguards whisked him off that she figured out he was a powerful man. So powerful, in fact, that nobody dared call him by his real name. Everybody in Stonehaven used his official title instead—The Mayor.

Shayna never slept with The Mayor, but he did manage to screw her on a business deal later on. It cost Shayna most of her insurance money and bruised her ego pretty good. They'd practically been at war ever since. Which was why Shayna and her crew were planning to rob The Mayor's house later that night.

But not before Shayna had her way with Edward. She walked slowly across the tiles, swaying her hips with every step she took. Then, when she was sure he was paying attention, she lingered in the bedroom doorway to let him admire the view. Soon the whoosh of rustling clothes filled the silence. If there was anything sexier than the sound of a sword hitting the tiles, Shayna didn't know what it was.

The diversion worked. The bikers went screaming off down the street once they heard that some of Shayna's pirates attacked one of their crew. With The Mayor out at a dinner meeting, that left his house unguarded.

Shayna led her men in through the kitchen door.

She'd been there a few times before, back when she and The Mayor were on better terms. So she knew exactly where his home office was. If he kept any of his stash here, that's where it would be.

Time was tight, so they quickly wound their way through the long hallways until they reached the door. Shayna twisted the knob and gave it a push. The room was dark and empty.

She waved the pirates inside while whispering orders.

"Start looking, but put everything back exactly where you found it. He doesn't need to know that we were even here."

They fanned out across the well-appointed space, carefully pulling books from the shelves and quietly sliding desk drawers open. Shayna joined a couple of her men that were looking for a safe behind one of the enormous, framed paintings that lined the paneled walls. It seemed like an eternity before one of them finally found what they were looking for.

All of the men quickly crowded around the safe to see if they could crack it, but Shayna's eyes were on the opposite wall. She spotted something hanging there that she hadn't noticed before. It was a framed map that reminded her of the one she'd stolen in New Orleans.

The Mayor's map was much larger than the one

from Keely's, but there was a piece missing in the middle. It was a jagged, saw-shaped hole that looked awfully familiar to her. She immediately snatched it down to study the markings, failing to hide the smile that spread across her face.

Shayna woke up before dawn the next morning. She rolled to the left, running her fingers across Edward's hairy chest. For a brief moment she imagined that it was Tommy Ruzzo lying beside her. Shayna reveled in the memory before shaking it from her head. She shimmied across the satin sheets, sliding to the floor.

She was still exhausted from the previous night's adventures. And not just the escapades after her bath, but the break-in that led her to the other half of Lafitte's map. Her lips curled into a small grin as she pictured it under the bed where Edward was currently sleeping.

Shayna stumbled across the bedroom, searching for her clothes on the floor. Edward's black-and-white striped T-shirt was all she could find. It barely reached the middle of her thighs, but it was better than nothing. *I'd prefer to stay naked if this damned house wasn't so cold in the mornings.*

She slipped from the bedroom and moved down

the hallway. The paneled walls were as bare as the day she and her crew moved in. They'd only been at this location for a few months, but she was already itching to relocate. Nothing outside of Florida ever kept Shayna happy for very long. Not even eight horny pirates could do the trick.

It was fun dressing up like a wench, and even more fun getting undressed by her favorite pirate every night, but Shayna wasn't suddenly into cosplay. She saw an opportunity with Edward and the others, a chance to move on with her life. If she couldn't bring herself to settle down with Tommy Ruzzo in Florida, then she wanted to immerse herself in another life all together. Her dedication to this new reality was so complete that she immediately took Edward from the street corner to the local spotlight.

They had started with a floating nightclub called Aurora's Galley that offered expensive bar food served by abusive pirate actors. A half-scale recreation of Captain Aurora's famous frigate, The Black Cutlass, the place had a small stage that they used for the occasional concertina band. Shayna had gone to the club's owner, The Mayor, and convinced him to let her start booking the place. Edward soon became the centerpiece for a nightly act that featured multiple Captain Aurora impersonators doing skits on stage all at once.

Those were the good old days, she thought, making her way to the living room. Flickering light from a muted TV greeted her as she entered. It sat on top of a wooden treasure chest pushed against the far wall. She snatched the remote, killing it. Almost every flat surface in the small room was covered with sleeping men—from the shabby sofa and love seat, to the battered coffee table and stained rug. In between, the landscape was littered with empty liquor bottles and a stuffed parrot or two. She wrinkled her nose at the smell of stale sweat polluting the air. It might have been the aftermath of a battle at sea, if it weren't for all the snoring.

Shayna never could have guessed in a million years that finding Edward on the streets would lead to all of this. Word of their bawdy performances at Aurora's Galley had begun to spread after months of perfecting the act. Reservations were selling out weeks in advance and lines were forming hours before showtime. Shayna had made good money from her cut of the bar, but a killing from the cocaine the actors dealt on the side.

Business was so good that she had used all of her insurance settlement to buy the business outright. The Mayor was more than happy to sell after a little coaxing from Shayna, but on one condition—no more drugs. He didn't have a moral issue with the narcotics trade; he just wanted to control all the profits from it in Stonehaven. It was an easy promise to keep. *For a few weeks, at least.*

Shayna stepped carefully over the bodies as she walked across the living room. The front door was open a crack, letting a thin sliver of pale morning light in through the screen. There was comfort in knowing that all of her men had made it home again. She was everything to them—mother, dealer and boss. Shayna laughed at the thought. *A terrible boss is more like it.*

The crowds at Aurora's Galley shrank soon after Shayna took ownership. It had turned out the restaurant was a money pit that The Mayor had been trying to unload for years. Once Shayna and her crew showed up, he finally saw a way out. From that point forward, he did everything in his power to artificially fill out the crowds. That initially included offering free food and drinks to busloads of tourists, and eventually extended to hiring friends and relatives to fill empty seats. Of course, Shayna didn't find any of this out until after she'd spent all of her money to buy the place.

Pretty soon it was really only the cocaine that was keeping the business afloat. So she brought in a bigger shipment from Miami the next time around. Problem was The Mayor brought in an even larger shipment of his own, and it had arrived a lot faster than Shayna's. Soon the streets were flooded with coke and the price was plummeting.

Shayna was furious that the same man had outsmarted her twice, so she began plotting her revenge. Namely, stealing that new shipment from The Mayor. It was a perfect plan because she could add to her own stash while destroying the competition at the same time. But that had all changed when she found The Mayor's map.

Shayna shook her head in disbelief at the memory. It already felt like a hundred years ago as she stood there among the pirates the next morning. She tried to enjoy the stillness for a moment because she knew another battle was brewing. Felt it in her bones.

The first shot came in the form of a creaking noise out on the porch. She hoped it was stray cats, but knew better. Her suspicions were confirmed when she pushed the screen door open and saw The Mayor in one of the rocking chairs.

"Good morning, Shayna. I didn't expect you'd be up for a few more hours."

He lifted his pork pie hat, arching an eyebrow. The top of his head was pasty and bald, but pointy tufts of brown hair jutted out above his ears. Shayna always thought it looked like a small football was lodged in his abnormally round skull.

She scanned the perimeter of the yard to assess the situation. His goons were hulking silhouettes in the background that all looked the same to her. Their cartoonish biker garb was no less ridiculous than the pirate outfits her men wore, only without the flare. What they lacked in imagination, they more than made up for in brutality.

Shayna pulled the end of her shirt down in feigned modesty. She'd take it off all together if she thought it would help.

"Hello, Mayor. What brings you out here so early on a weekend morning?"

Her voice was sweet, but her teeth were clenched. He rocked the chair forward to stand. His thick arms bulged in the sleeves of his striped seersucker jacket as he yawned and stretched. She could never quite make sense of his long torso and short legs. He was easily the ugliest person that Shayna had ever met, both inside and out.

"Can I get you a cup of coffee, or maybe a slice of pie?"

Shayna bit her lip, waiting to see if flirting would help.

"I'll have to pass." He patted his gut and winked. "I'm here on business."

She leaned against the doorjamb with folded arms, relieved that the pleasantries were over. Her voice had a razor-sharp edge now.

"City business or personal business?"

"A little of both, I'm afraid. I know we have to tolerate outsiders like you coming to visit our little town, but that doesn't mean you can steal from me."

"I have no idea what you're talking about."

He choked up a laugh. It was somewhere between a snort and a chuckle.

"I had my police chief do a little digging on you. You've got quite a colorful past. I'm certain I could have you arrested at any moment, but I think you deserve much worse than that."

Shayna didn't flinch, but inside she was squirming. She'd fooled herself that her past was dead and buried in Seatown. Any plans she'd made for the future would have to be accelerated now.

"What's stopping you?"

"For the moment, you've got something of mine and I want it back."

"Care to enlighten me?"

Smiles come easy to a politician, but they always looked pained on The Mayor.

"You broke into my house and stole a family heirloom."

Images of The Mayor's house flickered through her head. Shayna was so lost in her memories of the previous night that she almost forgot The Mayor was standing right in front of her. She managed to produce a shy smile that she hoped would reinforce her claims of ignorance.

"Hmm. Seems like whoever took this heirloom of yours knew what they were after. I'd probably hold onto it, if it was me. Might give me some leverage."

"For now. But there's more than one way to skin a cat." He turned, as if he was going to leave, but stopped. "Oh, by the way, I had a little chat with one of your men this morning."

Shayna resisted the urge to look over her shoulder into the living room. She didn't want to give him the satisfaction. *They were all there a minute ago, right?*

Her eyes were still on her unwanted guest when he lifted his bloody hand. It looked like he'd recently eaten barbecued ribs.

"I did most of the talking, of course." He pulled a handkerchief from his pocket, carefully cleaning his fingers one by one. "You really should lock your doors at night. This town is still full of pirates."

She yanked the screen door open as her guest stepped from the porch. The Mayor had already reached the sidewalk when Shayna saw what she'd missed before. Only six of the pirates were sleeping. The seventh one's neck had been snapped, his long beard covering the crooked evidence. She started screaming for help as she bent down to check his pulse. Edward came rushing in at the sound of her voice. He knelt down beside her.

"What the hell happened?"

The Mayor was whistling a sea shanty as he strolled away down the street. He stopped to call her name.

"Shayna! I'll be out of town on business until tomorrow. I expect everything will be back in its proper place when I return."

There wasn't much time to mourn. Shayna's remaining crew wrapped the corpse in a plastic tarp and duct-taped the ends while she ran back to the bedroom. She fished Lafitte's relic out from under her bed, smashing it open. Shards of broken glass fell to the floor as she carefully pulled the parchment out. It came as some surprise when a shiny stone rolled out behind it. She snatched the gem up and noticed a tiny scrap of paper beneath it.

Shayna pulled the note open. She had to read the scrawled message several times before it finally made sense.

"If found, please return to…"

Shayna's eyes went wide. She shoved the gem and the note into her pocket and went back to matching the maps. Putting those two pieces together—seeing that they were a perfect fit—was the biggest thrill she'd had since killing her husband.

She ran back into the living room. Her crew had already shoved the body into the chest the TV was sitting on before. Seven pirates walking down the street with a treasure chest might be suspicious in most towns, but not in Stonehaven.

They were headed to Aurora's Galley with their fallen mate that morning. There was no easy place to bury a body in Stonehaven, especially in broad daylight. But Shayna figured they could get rid of it by filling a chest with rocks and dumping the weighty cargo into the Sound. It wasn't exactly Davy Jones' Locker, but it would do in a pinch.

One of the pirates unlocked the gate on the dock and they all went up the gangplank. The sickening odor of rotting food greeted them as they walked into the dining room. Every one of them was a passable actor and a highly motivated drug dealer, but none of them liked to clean—least of all Shayna. She was amazed that they managed to keep the restaurant charade up at all.

"Stow the chest until we get out to sea, and clean this place up a little. I'll be in the office."

The men groaned as she descended a spiral staircase in the corner. It led to a spacious room that might have been a replica of Captain Aurora's sleeping chambers. These days it was filled with cardboard beer boxes, empty kegs and rolling racks full of pirate costumes. An ornate wooden desk was pushed into one corner, backlit by heavy brass wall lights. Shayna plopped down into her stuffed leather chair and waited.

Satisfied that she was alone, she opened her bag and pulled out the maps. She studied the hand-written symbols and loping script, even though she already had it memorized. The words that mattered most were written right across the top: "Here be the Treasure of Captain Aurora."

Shayna took her phone out, snapped a picture of the map and emailed it to herself. She opened the attachment on her desktop computer and printed a photo-quality image. She opened the top drawer on the desk, sliding the document between two pieces of glass. The drawer had a false bottom and a secret compartment where she usually kept what little cash they made from the restaurant. She tucked the backup copy of Aurora's map inside, making sure to lock it tight. The small key always dangled from a slender gold chain around her neck.

She almost jumped through the low ceiling when Edward cleared his throat on the other side of the desk.

"Jesus! You scared the crap out of me."

"Sorry, m'lady. It's—"

"Spit it out. We've got a busy day ahead of us."

"I was wondering if there's anything you wanted to tell me about what happened at the house this morning?"

Shayna stood up to walk around the desk. She didn't stop until their noses were inches apart.

"It's just business, Edward. You understand?"

"Aye, m'lady."

"Knock it off with the pirate act. Do you understand me or not?"

Her eyes glowed in the amber light. Edward's voice cracked.

"Aye—I mean, *yes.*"

"Good, because we need to kick our plan into high gear."

"You mean—?"

"Yes. Our time in Stonehaven is almost up. Trust me for a little while longer."

Shayna pulled open the desk drawer, producing a small metal wallet. It looked like a polished cigarette case with a lock on one side. She reached over to place it in his hand.

"Hold onto this for me. There is something very important inside. Keep it on you at all times, but don't look inside."

"Aye aye, m'lady."

DEAD MEN TELL NO TALES

It was almost one in the morning when Ruzzo stumbled back down the dock. He groped at the side of Mikey's boat in the dark until he found the rope ladder. There was always a chance that he would break his neck climbing aboard, but that might be a relief. There was nowhere else for him to live, and he couldn't be sober and be on the boat where he'd almost died. Especially without Shayna.

Ruzzo desperately wanted to go inside and sleep, but he had a ritual to complete first. He walked around the cabin to the far side of the boat, stopping when he reached his usual spot. It was a nondescript length of rail that wouldn't mean anything to anybody but him. It was where he'd been shot that fateful night, and where his attacker had gone overboard—never to be seen again.

His legs were a little unsteady as he brought his zipper down. There had been plenty of nights when he'd woken up on the deck with his pants around his ankles, so he had to be vigilant. The familiar sound of piss hitting the water below was reassuring. It was soon drowned out by his own screaming.

"I'm gonna find you, Cavanaugh! You miserable bastard!"

Ruzzo finished up, packing away his tackle. The cabin was pitch black when he walked in. He groped in the dark for the desk lamp, finding a half-empty bottle of rum instead. His gun was right there beside it on the desk. The light suddenly didn't seem so important anymore.

He stumbled backwards into a wooden captain's chair with a crash. His right hand seemed to have a mind of its own as he brought the bottle up. The rum was sweet on his lips. He took a second gulp and let the bottle drop into his lap. Now he brought his left hand up. The barrel of the gun felt cold against his temple, like a numbing piece of ice. He pulled the trigger and listened to the hollow click. *Maybe I'll have better luck tomorrow night.*

Ruzzo was still in the same chair when he woke up the next morning. Somebody was standing over him, lightly slapping his face.

"You've got a visitor, Ruzzo."

Seagulls shrieked in the sky outside. Ruzzo tried to force his eyes open, but the soft morning light burned like fire. A tepid glass of water thrown in his face did the trick.

Ruzzo leapt from the chair at the rude awakening. He bounced off of Sgt. Badeaux's chest and tumbled to the floor.

"Christ! What the hell's wrong with you?"

"I'm getting tired of all your tough guy phone messages. Thought I'd come and talk it out with you, man to man."

Ruzzo rubbed his eyes, looking up at the familiar trooper hat and mirrored sunglasses. Nothing had changed about Sgt. Badeaux since the day they'd met. He dropped a copy of *The Seatown Sentinel* on the floor at Ruzzo's feet. It was folded to the back page.

"You still addicted?"

Ruzzo snorted.

"Yep, but not to crossword puzzles."

Sgt. Badeaux reached out to help him stand. Ruzzo lunged for the bottle of rum, but Sgt. Badeaux slapped his hand away.

"That can wait until we're done. You got any coffee?"

"Only instant. You'll have to boil some water."

"No, thanks. That stuff tastes like crap."

Ruzzo chuckled.

"You've got refined tastes for a redneck."

"And you smell like ten feet of wide open ass."

It was Sgt. Badeaux's turn to smile now. Ruzzo gave his own armpits a theatrical sniff and shrugged.

"You don't like it, feel free to leave."

"Simmer down. I'm here on police business."

Sgt. Badeaux took a seat at the table. He slid the bottle and Ruzzo's gun out of reach.

"Either one will kill you."

Ruzzo dropped into a seat. It took everything in him not to throw up as he stared Sgt. Badeaux down. Ruzzo caught his own reflection in the cabin's window, barely recognizing himself. His pasty scowl was distorted by bloat and hate.

"Thanks for the public service announcement. Mind telling me why you're here?"

Sgt. Badeaux sighed. His disappointment and disgust were obvious.

"What the hell happened to you, Ruzzo? I thought you wanted to get back on the force."

Ruzzo struck back, his response dripping with sarcasm.

"I gave up on that plan when I realized I could never be a better cop than you. Is that what you came here to ask me?"

Sgt. Badeaux shook his head in surrender.

"We're calling off the manhunt for Cavanaugh."

Ruzzo slammed his fist down on the table. It felt like the veins in his forehead would burst. The gun bounced a few inches closer.

"The fuck you are!"

The louder Ruzzo got, the quieter Sgt. Badeaux's response.

"We can, and we will. There hasn't been a single sighting of him since—"

"Since he shot me! You also never found a body."

"Calm down, Ruzzo. We'll still follow up on any leads we get. I think it's best that we all move on with our lives. Especially you."

That's exactly what Ruzzo was afraid of. As long as he had Cavanaugh to focus on, he didn't have to face up to the fact that he was a wreck. Or that Cavanaugh wasn't the only one who had completely disappeared from his life.

Sgt. Badeaux stood up, taking his sunglasses off. It took his eyes a second to focus in the dim light.

"You heard anything from Shayna?"

It was hard to hear her name without wanting to commit murder. Ruzzo somehow fought the urge to jump out of his chair and strangle Sgt. Badeaux. It would just be another form of suicide in his current state, no better or worse than what was already on the table beside him.

"If you've got something to tell me, spit it out."

Ruzzo tried to swallow the hope in his voice. His pride wouldn't allow him to exhibit any more weakness than was already on display. Sgt. Badeaux strolled over to the door, chewing on his thoughts.

"Got an interesting call from the New Orleans PD, now that you mention it."

Ruzzo leaned forward, involuntarily scooting to the edge of his chair. He'd never let his guard down so far before. Sgt. Badeaux studied him for a moment before going on.

"I'll be damned, bubba. That's the most alive I've seen you look in a year."

"And your point is...?"

"If you had a tail, it'd be wagging up a storm about now."

Sgt. Badeaux slid his sunglasses on before stepping outside.

"They had some questions about a woman who was staying there a while back. Said she might be a witness in an arson investigation at some bar called Keely's. Ever heard of that place?"

Ruzzo was stunned silent. The most he could do was shake his head. Sgt. Badeaux tipped his hat, stepped outside.

"That's kind of what I thought you'd say."

Ruzzo watched his guest leave while blindly groping for the bottle of rum. His hand landed on the gun instead. He lifted it up, studying the weapon in his hand. It was the first time in months that he didn't want to turn it on himself.

SHARK BAIT

Aurora's Galley wasn't much to look at, but she was seaworthy. And a few of Shayna's men grew up in Stonehaven, so they knew how to pretend they were sailing. The boat was actually powered by a couple of high-powered motors attached to the stern. It didn't hurt that the reduced scale made her crew look like giants when they stood on the deck.

Rumor had it that Captain Aurora buried untold riches in the vicinity of Stonehaven prior to meeting his fate on nearby Corcoran Island in 1718. Professional treasure hunters and locals alike had been searching for the loot ever since, with absolutely no success. But that didn't stop the hoards from swarming the local beaches every summer with their mail-order metal detectors and scoop shovels. While other, more sophisticated operations came to town with expensive diving gear, sonar equipment, and complicated geological data. They all went home rich with experience, but deeper in debt.

Shayna laughed out loud thinking about how many people had failed to find the treasure. She studied the map as they swung wide of the harbor town of Corcoran, heading instead for an uninhabited stretch of beach further north. That's where a small arrow on the map pointed to a rocky cove. A dotted line wound up along the white sand beach from there, and into the island's interior.

"Land ho!" Edward cried thirty minutes later. They hadn't been out of sight of land for the last hour and a half, but Shayna thought it was a nice touch. She rolled the map up and carefully slipped it into her shoulder bag to prepare for their arrival. The only other items she had with her were a phone, a vial of cocaine, a small pistol, and a silver bracelet that doubled as a knife. Her men would be carrying the shovels and picks they'd need to unearth the treasure once they found it.

But first they had to navigate the giant rock formations that sent violent sprays of ocean water into the air all around them. She turned to Edward and gave him a slap on the shoulder.

"Did you throw the trunk overboard?"

"Yarrrrrrr, m'lady!"

"In that case, it's showtime."

She winked and spun away. It only took a few strides before she reached two more of her men. They were passing a bottle of rum back and forth between them. She snatched it by the neck and took a long pull. The pirates cheered when she brought it back down again, letting loose with a loud belch.

"Ready for a little adventure?"

"Aye aye, m'lady!"

She slapped one of them on the ass before moving on. It wasn't long before she'd given each of her crew a little confidence boost. For some it was a peck on the cheek, while others got a close up peek at her pushed up cleavage. The extra loyalty would come in handy when she was making them dig hole after hole throughout the night. It didn't hurt that she'd also promised each man five percent of the haul.

Another hour passed before they lowered a skiff and started rowing for the island. The small vessel was heavy with bodies and equipment so the going was slow. It was close to dusk when they finally splashed ashore.

A certain pride welled up in Shayna's chest as she watched the crew working together on her plan. She stopped to take a drink of water, her eyes scanning the horizon. Two tall palm trees in the distance bent in the wind, crossing each other to form an X. It wasn't on the map in Shayna's bag, but she thought it was a good sign anyway.

* * *

The moon hung heavy in the sky when they finally reached their destination. Shayna and her crew followed every clue on the map until they reached a small clearing near the northern tip of the island. It was a couple of miles from the port where ferries transported tourists to the Outer Banks, but obscured by a thick stand of oak trees. The men were too exhausted to feign enthusiasm when she told them they had reached their destination. They simply dropped their gear to the ground and collapsed nearby.

"Edward. Give these men something to eat, and the rum we brought."

"As you wish, m'lady."

He went over to his backpack to distribute the meager supplies. Beef jerky and Bacardi might not be a feast, but it would help to get them through the night. Edward was carrying a couple packs of cigarettes and the vial of cocaine in her bag was only meant to be broken out if things got desperate.

Shayna caught Edward's eye. She had him hold the map between them while she lit it up with the screen of her phone.

"See these shapes right here? I think it's those hills over there. And these circles are those boulders."

He frowned in response. She wasn't in the mood for pantomime.

"What?"

"There are more circles on the map then boulders over there."

"A lot can change in three hundred years."

He pretended to shrug it off, but Shayna could tell he was annoyed. She tried to focus his attention back on the map.

"If we're here, then the treasure…"

She slid her finger down the parchment until it reached the skull and crossbones symbol. *Or "crossed bones," as Lafitte would say.*

It was impossible to tell from the hand-drawn map how much area it covered in the real world.

"…is right here."

They both turned around to look at the empty space behind them. The field was about fifty yards across, and easily twice as long. It was going to be a long night.

"All right you lazy bastards, time to get to work. First man who touches their shovel to the treasure chest gets double their share of the booty."

All six men jumped to their feet. Shayna had Edward break them into three teams of two. That way they could cover more ground at once. They spread out in a triangle formation about twenty yards apart and started digging. The sound of shovels splitting the earth reverberated around the empty space.

Shayna left Edward to supervise the men while she did a little exploring. Those palm trees she'd spotted from the beach were nearby now, hard to miss since they didn't grow wild in the Outer Banks. She wound through a grove of twisted oaks that lined the eastern edge of the field. It didn't take long to find what she was looking for.

She noticed right away that the palm trees hadn't blown together—they were tied that way. X definitely marked the spot, but it wasn't left by any eighteenth century pirates. A private landing strip stretched out from the base of the tree trunks for several hundred yards. She followed the narrow runway to a corrugated steel hanger.

There were only a few windows, but they were blacked out from the inside. Even standing on an oil drum and pressing her face to the glass did no good. Shayna jumped down and went around to the large, sliding doors. They were chained securely, like she knew they would be. She was looking around for something heavy to break the pad locks when a gunshot cracked in the distance.

Shayna dropped everything and ran back to where her men were digging. She arrived in time to see one of The Mayor's goons bring a shovel down across a pirate's head. The biker laughed as the bearded man fell in a bloody heap. She reached into her bag for the pistol, as a familiar *click* sounded from behind.

Edward stood there with his gun leveled.

"Sorry, Shayna. It's just business."

She looked over his shoulder to where The Mayor emerged from the darkness. A familiar pained smile spread across his face like a knife wound.

"I thought I might run into you out here tonight."

The Mayor nodded to the biker with the shovel. He lifted the makeshift weapon, bringing it down again and again until the pirate at his feet stopped moving. Nobody said a word while the metal blade pinged against the dead man's skull. The slaughter seemed to last for a hundred years.

Shayna tried to avert her eyes, but The Mayor grabbed her by the hair.

"I want you to see what you've done. These men trusted you, but you let them down. And for what? A silly treasure map."

He pushed her to the ground, shoving the gun under her chin.

"People have dug up every inch of this island

and nobody—especially not some Florida whore—has ever found any buried treasure."

Shayna's voice was defiant.

"Then why's that map mean so much to you?"

He lifted his chin, releasing a laugh into the chilly ocean air. His eyes caught the moonlight when he brought them back down.

"Because it belonged to my daddy. Only idiots like him believe in buried treasure, you stupid bitch."

The Mayor brought his gun up, aiming at two other members of Shayna's crew.

"You either come work for me now, or you die right here."

The pirates turned to look at their captain. Tears rolled down Shayna's cheeks now.

"Do what he says."

The remaining pirates all went over to stand behind the bikers. The Mayor turned back to address her again. It sounded like she was being teased on the playground by one of the mean girls in elementary school.

"Looks like you're running out of men, fast."

"You got what you wanted. Shoot me and get it over with."

"What's the fun in that?"

He reached down, yanking the map from her hands.

"I don't know how you got your hands on the second half of this map, but it's going to cost you dearly."

The Mayor waved two of his men over.

"Take her out to Aurora's Galley, tie her to the mast, and send them both down to the ocean floor."

Shayna screamed and tried to break free. The Mayor made a disappointed clucking sound in response.

"I thought you'd be pleased with my creativity. Seems like a fitting death for a pirate queen."

Shayna's outfit was tattered and dripping as she crawled ashore, clutching a trash bag in her hand. She stumbled a few yards up the sand and collapsed in a sodden heap. The folds of the plastic rustled beside her in the breeze as she passed out.

A few hours later the sun was poking up over the trees to the west, but she couldn't stop shivering. It wasn't because she was cold.

Shayna sat up to tear the bag open. She pushed the copy of the map aside and snatched her phone up. Her eyes wander across the expanse of water that spread out before her. It was hard to imagine that Aurora's Galley was beneath it all, and that she was supposed to be with it. The Mayor's men had done everything right, except they forgot to check her jewelry. That bracelet with the knife inside had really come in handy once the boat finally started going down.

She lifted the phone to look at the screen. There was one bar of reception that kept flickering in and out. The battery still had a five percent charge, but it wouldn't last long. It was now or never.

Shayna scrolled through her contacts again, even though she had the number memorized. There was still nobody else that she could think to call. Not a single other person in the entire world who could get her out of this mess. At least nobody who was still alive.

She tapped out the ten digits, letting her thumb hover over the *Call* button. There was nothing she wanted more at the moment than to hear his voice. He would drop everything he was doing and come to rescue her, no matter how great the danger. That's the kind of man Tommy Ruzzo was, but her heart still couldn't risk getting him killed.

She dropped the phone to the ground. *If he's meant to come save me, than the universe can send him the message.*

HOIST THE MIZZEN

Ruzzo was cleaning a fish. He brought the blade down with a thud, separating the silvery head from its body. One dead eye stared up at him, boring into his mind and judging him for every bad decision he'd ever made. The staring contest stretched for a long moment before Ruzzo flicked the head away with the tip of his knife. He picked his can of beer up, pouring the last of the warm liquid into his mouth.

Keeping Mikey company during weekend fishing trips was a condition of living on the boat. It wasn't easy for Ruzzo out there, especially when the water got rough, but it was the least he could do. His friend was always happy and relaxed when they were out to sea. That's why he waited until they were back at the dock before dropping the information he'd been holding back. He wanted to have one more day like that before he said goodbye.

"I've made some decisions about a few things."

Mikey popped a beer open, taking a seat.

"I hope you aren't about to ask me for a raise."

"This is the opposite of that."

"What the hell's the opposite of a raise? Are you giving money back?"

"What? No. Shut up and hear me out."

Ruzzo ran a hand across his hair, searching for the right words. The truth was that he'd never quit a job before. They'd always just ended—some fizzled, while others imploded—much like his relationships. He was terrible at drawn out goodbyes.

"It's like this. I've been in Florida long enough. I need to get out while I still can."

"So you're going back to New York with your tail between your legs?"

Ruzzo set the fillet knife down, wiping his hands on a gummy bar towel.

"Actually, no. I'm heading to New Orleans. I heard Shayna might be there."

Ruzzo mumbled that last comment. Mikey clammed up at the mention of her name. A blank expression washed over his sunburned face as he worked through it in his head. Ruzzo gave him time. He knew that if anybody understood what she meant to him, it was Mikey. He was probably the only real friend Ruzzo had left.

A full minute passed before Mikey slammed his bottle down on the table.

"I'm coming with you."

Whatever response Ruzzo had been expecting, this wasn't it.

"What are you talking about? You have a business to run, right here in Seatown."

"I've got people working for me that can hold down the fort. Besides, I haven't had a vacation in years."

"I'm not sure you would do much relaxing on this trip—"

"You worry about Shayna. I can relax almost anywhere."

Mikey folded his arms tight, signaling that there would be no further discussion about it. Ruzzo obliged, happy that he would have somebody to rely on if things got rough. *Things always do when Shayna's involved.*

And it didn't hurt that Mikey owned a truck. Ruzzo smiled.

"When will you be ready to leave?"

"Let's have a farewell party tonight and take off in the morning. I think you're gonna like my ride."

Mikey's "ride" was a jacked up four-by-four truck with enormous knobby wheels, a gun rack in the rear window, and what sounded like a jet engine under the hood. It had been a chore climbing up into the passenger seat, but the view from the cab was spectacularly unobstructed.

Ruzzo's hands were planted firmly on the dash-board while Mikey bobbed and weaved his way through mid-morning traffic. Marilyn Manson's "Beautiful People" was the latest in a string of nineties alternative rock abominations that Mikey blasted at him. It was cold comfort, but Ruzzo was almost thankful for Mikey's off-key warbling.

Ruzzo had other things to worry about anyway. He wouldn't be surprised if they eventually rolled over one of the compact cars that they were tail-gating. Mikey whooped when the latest one turned its blinker on, moving over to the right.

"Get the hell out of my way, little man!"

Ruzzo gave a sideways glance to the beer bottle between his driver's legs, wondering if this had been the best decision after all. Mikey lifted it up in a toast, screaming to be heard over the revving motor and music.

"You sure you don't want one? You look like shit."

"I'll stick with coffee."

Their long night at the bar spilled over onto the boat. The sun was almost up by the time they finally passed out. That meant both of them were run-ning on less than two hours of sleep with a long drive ahead. If the first thirty minutes were any indication, it wasn't going to be an easy trip. More than anything, Ruzzo wanted to get there so he could know for sure if Shayna was still around. He wasn't holding his breath.

They pulled over at a gas station that was surrounded on three sides by swampland. Ruzzo jumped out of the truck, heading straight for the bathroom. The walls above the urinal were covered in ballpoint-pen graffiti. Most of the pictures were so badly drawn that he had to squint to see what they were supposed to be. The writing beside one caught his eye: "For good head call Shayna." The number wasn't familiar, but he put his fist through the wall anyway. *There's probably a thousand girls in Florida named Shayna.*

His knuckles were still aching when he climbed back up into the truck. There were two plastic bags on the seat between them now. It looked like Mikey had bought one of everything in the convenience store. Beef jerky, cupcakes, potato chips, cigarettes, forty-ounce bottles of malt liquor, chocolate milk, energy drinks and a selection of several different candy bars spilled out at Ruzzo's feet.

He almost couldn't believe his eyes.

"You know this is only a five hour drive, right?"

"This is how you road trip, Florida-style. You need to chill."

Mikey turned the stereo up. The window in Ruzzo's door was vibrating in time to Limp Bizkit as they swerved back onto the highway.

"Can you at least turn the music down?"

The volume didn't budge, but Mikey started screaming even louder.

"What are you going to do when she's not there?"

Ruzzo's chest tightened. He knew it was a possibility—maybe even an inevitability—but he wasn't willing to admit it. That's a bridge he would cross when he got there.

"I'll keep looking until I find her."

Ruzzo felt good saying the words that had been eating at him. He leaned his head back and closed his eyes.

Shayna was waiting for him when he did. They were back on the beach together, naked and rolling around on a blanket. He could feel the warmth of a bonfire burning on his back as she dug her nails in. The heat grew more intense until it became unbearable. Ruzzo rolled onto his side and saw that there was a house on fire nearby. He jumped up to help the firefighters put it out, but Shayna kept pulling him back down to the sand. She grabbed at his hands and clawed at his legs, begging him not to go. He couldn't stop himself—he needed to go and help. It was his duty to go help.

A solid punch to the arm woke him from his dreams. Ruzzo shook his head, forcing his eyes open. He saw Mikey smiling back at him when he did. His cheeks were flush and his eyes were practically crossed. The floor at his feet was littered with empty beer bottles and tiny energy shot bottles.

Mikey was shitfaced. Meanwhile, the world outside whizzed by them at a hundred miles an hour.

"Wakey, wakey. We're almost there."

It took a lot of convincing, but Ruzzo eventually got Mikey to let him drive. His partner was the one passed out in the passenger seat now while Ruzzo tried to maneuver the monstrous vehicle. Any other redneck on that stretch of road must have been scratching their head when they saw him doing the speed limit in the slow lane.

Ruzzo was thankful for the tinted windows. He felt like a little old lady behind the controls of a tank. The only thing keeping him sane was the Frank Sinatra playlist he had on the stereo now. He was whistling along to *Summer Wind* an hour later when he saw the first exit signs for New Orleans.

He pulled into a liquor store parking lot the minute they got into town. Mikey remained unconscious in the truck while Ruzzo went in to ask for directions to Keely's. The girl behind the counter seemed a little young to know where the bar was, but still managed to sketch out a map on the back of a paper bag. She raised an eyebrow when she pushed it across the counter to him.

"I heard that place burned down, mister."

"I know," Ruzzo responded in his best cop voice. "I'm actually here as part of the investigation."

It was a silly lie meant to impress a teenaged girl, but it felt good to pretend like he had any authority at all. He stood up a little taller and squared his shoulders to drive the point home. She took a look at his bulging gut, forcing an awkward smile. Ruzzo sucked it back in instinctively before backing out of the store.

He knew that he needed to become the man he used to be or Shayna wouldn't take him back—especially if he wanted her to move to New York with him. It wasn't going to be easy after all the time he spent getting drunk and doughy in Florida.

Mikey was gone when he got back to the truck. He jumped up onto the driver's side step to scan the parking lot. He didn't see Mikey in the immediate vicinity, but noticed a sign in the next parking lot over: "Drive-Thru Hurricanes." There was a long line of cars backed up into the street. They were honking at some unseen obstacle. Ruzzo ran over to find Mikey at the window trying to convince the server to sell him a drink. He was being pretty persistent, despite that fact that he was barefoot, shirtless and had no money.

Ruzzo grabbed his friend by the arm, marching him back to the truck. Acting like a cop was like riding a bike.

"Get back in your seat and buckle up. Keely's is only a mile or two from here."

Mikey rolled his eyes, giving a wobbly salute.

"Aye-aye, cap'n."

Ruzzo knew his partner would be useless for the rest of the night, unless he needed a battering ram.

"Buckle up. I don't want to get pulled over on our way over there."

He merged out into traffic. Ruzzo studied the hand-drawn map, carefully following the many com-plicated turns it described. It wasn't long before they pulled up outside of the burned-out shell of a building. A flimsy cyclone fence had been erected around the perimeter of the property. The windows were boarded up, and the charred front door hung at an angle. It looked like maybe somebody was still living inside. *If New Orleans was anything like New York, it's probably junkies.*

Ruzzo punched the steering wheel. The sudden flurry of activity momentarily snapped Mikey out of his stupor.

"What the hell did you expect?"

"I expected you to keep your shit together, for starters."

"Go to hell. I'm on vacation."

Ruzzo grabbed his Smith & Wesson from the glove compartment, jumping from the truck before saying anything else. He edged around the gleaming front fender, taking in Keely's as he walked. Whatever the place had once been, it was now waiting to be torn down. He slipped through a gap in the chain link fence and headed for the porch. The yard was covered in piles of burnt furniture and singed pirate décor. He didn't see the shotgun poking out from behind the front door until it was too late.

His heart skipped a beat when a woman's voice yelled out, and almost broke when he realized it wasn't Shayna's.

"What the hell do you want?"

He stopped in his tracks, putting on his best negotiation voice. Tough, but calm—like they'd taught him at the academy.

"I'm here looking for a friend. Her name's Shayna Bil—"

The buckshot went high, whizzing over Ruzzo's

head as he dove behind a pile of empty beer kegs for cover. He heard somebody talking inside the building as the dust settled around him. It sounded like a lover's quarrel.

Ruzzo pulled the gun from the back of his pants, rolling over onto his stomach. The front door was in plain view now. He had it in his sights when the yelling started again. It was a man's voice this time.

"Shayna ain't here, but we can tell you where she went."

Definitely fucking junkies.

Ruzzo patted his pocket to make sure he had cash on him. There's one thing he knew for sure, junkies are always for sale. It was the quality of the information you had to be worried about.

"How much is it going to cost me?"

The man started to yell a hundred, but the woman screamed over him.

"Three hundred!"

Ruzzo only had sixty on him, but that would be more than enough to get what he needed.

"You've got a deal. Throw your gun onto the porch and come out where I can see you."

There was a moment of silence followed by a flurry of hushed chatter.

"You a cop?"

The man's voice was less sure now. Ruzzo didn't hesitate.

"You want the money or not?"

The gun came clattering out onto the porch. A sneaker emerged from behind the door first, connected to a thin man with spiky blond hair. Ruzzo took inventory of his filthy clothes and stubbly, gaunt face. The man stood up and held his hands out. Ruzzo didn't move an inch.

"What about the woman?"

The man on the porch looked over his shoulder, whispering something into the darkened bar. She crawled out behind him, struggling to squeeze through the narrow space. Ruzzo jumped up to level his gun, but kept his distance.

"Step down onto the lawn."

They did as they were told. He seemed eager, but she was reluctant. Ruzzo fished the money from his pocket, holding it up for them to see.

"That's far enough. Tell me what you know."

The man cleared his throat, but Ruzzo cut him off. He swung his gun to point at the woman.

"You've done enough talking. I want to hear from your girlfriend."

She folded her arms, glaring.

"Shayna worked here for a little while, but she's been gone a long time now."

The woman spat at the ground, apparently disgusted at having to speak her name. Ruzzo kept his expression neutral.

"Where'd she go?"

"Hell if I know, but she took something that belonged to us before she left."

"Oh yeah? What exactly?"

"That'll cost you extra."

If Ruzzo didn't know any better, he'd think she was buying time. He glanced over his shoulder, but only saw the truck parked there. Footsteps came thundering up when he turned back around. The baseball bat missed his head by less than an inch.

He ducked to the side and came up swinging. The handle of the Smith & Wesson caught his attacker in the side of the head. It made a sickly cracking sound that lingered in the air long after the body hit the ground. He took a step forward to get a better look at the goon who'd tried to brain him. His knees went wobbly when he saw it was a woman.

The man on the porch swooped in right at that moment. He snatched the cash from Ruzzo's hand and made a run for it, shimmying through the front gate like a feral cat. He was headed out into the street when the truck's passenger door swung open.

It sent the junkie back onto the sidewalk with a loud crunch. He was out cold.

Mikey stumbled out and gave the junkie a kick to the ribs for good measure. He had a proud smile on his face as Ruzzo brought the gun back around to the woman on the porch. They couldn't risk staying out in the open like this any longer.

"Any more surprises waiting for me inside?"

She went back into the bar with Ruzzo close behind. Mikey was already hiding the limp body out of sight of any nosy neighbors.

The inside of the place smelled like somebody pissed out a campfire. Every surface was scarred and charcoal black, including the wooden bar. Ruzzo was surprised to see a man sitting there sipping on a beer anyway. He had a black knit cap and a long white beard.

The woman went over to stand beside him.

"This is Lafitte. He'll tell you where that whore of yours went."

NOR'EASTER

Ruzzo and Mikey arrived in Stonehaven the next morning. It was a little closer to New York, but not close enough for Ruzzo's taste.

Ruzzo drove down Aurora Boulevard looking for a place to get some sleep. American flags alternated with Jolly Rogers on every streetlight down the main drag. He pulled into the first motel he found without a "No Vacancy" sign. The place was called the Yo Ho Hotel and it did not disappoint. It seemed like every business they passed was either named for Captain Aurora or had a pirate pun in the name. So far they'd seen the Shiver Me Timbers lumberyard, a chiropractor's office called Get Kraken, and an auto dealership named Billy's Used Carrrggghhhs.

This hotel went the extra mile by also looking like it was built in the era of that famous pirate. The front office was shaped like the prow of a ship while prop cannons lined the balconies. Mikey enjoyed the cheesy pirate theme a lot more than Ruzzo did.

"Did you see that restaurant back there? It's called The Jelly Roger!"

He was literally slapping his knee when Ruzzo threw the truck into park. Mikey wasn't blackout drunk, but he wasn't sober either. That left Ruzzo to drive the entire trip from New Orleans. He was brain dead and needed a shower.

"Stay here while I get us a room."

"Get two. I mean, in case I meet somebody and want to bring them back."

Mikey gave a theatrical wink. Ruzzo didn't think it was worth fighting over the extra room, especially if it meant he might get a real night's sleep.

"Fine."

He jumped down from the truck, shuffling over to the small lobby. His back ached in a way that it never had before. *Great. Now I'm getting creaky on top of everything else.*

Ruzzo rang the bell on the counter. Somebody called out from the back room a second later.

"I'll be out in a minute!"

Ruzzo grabbed a free newspaper from the stack by the door, taking a seat to wait. It was a local rag called *The Stonehaven Buccaneer*. It followed the same basic format as *The Seatown Sentinel*. He flipped to the crossword puzzle out of habit, before turning back to the front page. The largest headline was about a floating restaurant that recently sank off the coast.

That's as far as he got before the clerk appeared. He was so tall that he had to crouch down to be seen through the service window.

"Sorry about that. I ate something that disagreed with me."

The man patted his round stomach, grimacing as Ruzzo approached.

"So, need a room with one bed?"

"Two, actually."

"One room with two beds, or two rooms with two beds?"

He was a fast talker with a thick local accent. Ruzzo was having a hard time keeping up.

"Two singles."

"You're in luck, because we have those available. It'd be a totally different story if you came during the annual Pirate Festival. This town loses its mind during that week. You should come back and visit then. AARP?"

Ruzzo wasn't looking his best, but that question seemed out of line.

"I'm only thirty-three—"

"Yes, sorry. I meant your guest. Is he, or *she*, an AARP member? I only ask because you'd get a discount. Same with Triple A, although it wouldn't matter how old you were in that case."

"No. We'll pay the regular price."

"Your loss. The bar out by the pool is open until one, in case you want a nightcap."

The clerk started typing away, giving Ruzzo an occasional sideways glance. He stopped when he noticed the newspaper in Ruzzo's hand.

"Too bad about Aurora's Galley."

"Huh?"

The clerk pointed at the image on the front page.

"The floating restaurant."

"Oh, right. Yeah, it looks terrible."

"Damn shame about the woman who owned it. I hope the divers find her body in the wreckage so they can give her a proper burial. She was a real sweetheart—" The man stooped down to lean out the window. He brought his hands out in front of his chest for emphasis. "—if you know what I mean."

"I'm not from around here, so I wouldn't have any idea."

"Well, take my word for it. Shayna was one of a kind."

Ruzzo froze. The newspaper fell from his hands, floating to the floor.

"I'm sorry. What did you say her name was?"

"Shayna. Shayna Billups."

The clerk frowned, unsure what to make of Ruzzo's shocked expression.

"Are you a friend of hers or something?"

"I was."

Ruzzo couldn't sleep. Mikey, on the other hand, went out like a light—an incredibly drunk and belligerent light. Ruzzo listened to him snoring through the wall of their adjoining rooms all night.

He lay there in the dark, starring up at the cottage cheese ceiling, imagining what it would feel like to touch her. This was as close as he'd been to Shayna since she left him at the hospital in a drug-fueled haze a year ago—and now she was gone again. The possibility of seeing her, holding her in his arms and kissing those lips, was something he hadn't let himself consider up to that moment. Those fantasies alternated with the ones where she was bloated and eyeless at the bottom of the sound. He'd seen enough bodies recovered from the East River in Queens to know what fish could do.

It was close to two in the morning when Ruzzo finally gave up on sleep, going outside to clear his head instead. The air was cold and smelled of the ocean in way that Florida never did. Ruzzo stared at the neon blue, kidney-shaped pool. It took him a minute to notice a couple of drunks growling at each other in the dark.

They were two floors down, almost directly beneath where Ruzzo stood. One of them was smoking a cigarette that apparently kept dropping from between his fingers. He barked out a string of foul obscenities every time it happened.

Ruzzo leaned over the railing to take a closer look. Both men were wearing heavy black boots, blue jeans and denim jackets. Matching biker gang patches covered most of their backs. Their heads were shaved clean and their thick arms were covered in tattoos. The second man dwarfed the lounge chair he stood next to.

Ruzzo could hear every word they were saying now that he was paying attention.

"I don't trust the new guy. Why's The Mayor got such a hard on for him?"

"Who, Edward? Dude's a pussy. But if The Mayor likes him, we like him too."

"I'd like him better dead."

"Keep talking shit and you'll end up in the sound like Aurora's Galley."

One of them opened a fresh beer can. Ruzzo jumped back at the sudden cracking sound. His head hit the vending machine behind him with a loud *thunk*. He sat perfectly still, trying to be sure that the men hadn't heard him. They started talking again before he edged back over to the railing.

"Did you see the tits on that pirate bitch?"

"Every time I close my eyes."

"Too bad he made us off her. I would've liked to get a little taste of that."

"Well it ain't too late, if you don't mind swimming."

It took a minute before their laughter devolved into a series of stuttering grunts. There was a hint of doubt in the smaller man's voice when he cleared his throat to speak.

"I heard they still haven't found her body. You don't think she got away, do you?"

"No way in hell. I tied those knots myself. Let's get out of here."

Ruzzo tore down the stairs, taking them two and three at a time. The bikers were already out of sight when he reached the bottom. He sprinted across the parking lot and went left at the sidewalk. The two men were only a block ahead of him, making slow progress as they stumbled and weaved. He could picture his gun sitting on the nightstand, but knew there wasn't time to go back and grab it. Ruzzo was outnumbered, but he guessed he could take two drunks if he had to.

He slowed his pace anyway, hoping they'd lead

him to this "Mayor" they'd been speaking about. Whoever this biker chief was, it seemed like he held the key to finding Shayna. *If she's even alive.*

The two men crossed the street mid-block without looking back. Ruzzo kept walking straight ahead. He wanted to be sure they weren't setting some kind of trap for him. Experience taught him that tailing a suspect on foot was much more difficult than in a car. There were too many opportunities to get spotted, especially in the middle of the night when the streets were empty.

Ruzzo was parallel with the bikers when they turned down a narrow side street. He concentrated on their loud voices as they disappeared into the darkness. His plan was to wait until he reached the next corner before crossing over and doubling back. The men were already three blocks down when he picked up their trail again. He kept his distance, using the unlit side street as his cover.

They were moving a little faster now, as if the walk was burning off the alcohol. The small clapboard houses and white picket fences were giving way to larger parcels of land. There were only two or three properties per block by the time they were a mile off of Main Street. That's when Ruzzo saw one of the largest, most ornate homes he had ever encountered.

Glowing, yellow windows adorned every wall, green shudders held open at their sides. The peaked roofs and columned porches jutted upward and outward in every direction. The impressive, imposing structure rose up out of the gloom at the end of the street like every road in town had been designed to lead there.

Ruzzo hung back while the bikers wandered up the driveway and into a side door on the garage. The lights stayed on, but there was no more motion after that. He half expected to hear the roar of motorcycle engines, but guessed that the men had simply gone to bed instead. *Right there on the concrete floor like the animals they are.*

He gave it another minute or two before creeping forward. The house seemed to grow ten feet taller with every step he took, as if it were rising up to greet him. It was a couple of minutes before he reached the carriage doors on the garage. He stood up on his toes to peak in a window when he felt the cold metal against his neck.

The teeth of the massive knife blade bit at his skin. He could smell beer and cigarettes as a voice rasped in his ear.

"What took you so long, asshole?"

Ruzzo knew the biker wasn't looking for an answer, so he kept his mouth shut.

"That's what I thought. Come on."

He grabbed Ruzzo by the back of his shirt, shoving him toward the front door. His blade never left Ruzzo's neck, even as they climbed the stairs and went inside. The polished wooden floors glowed orange as they walked down the hallway and into the living room. Flames danced in a massive fireplace, flanked on either side by garish family portraits in gilded frames. Soft classical music seemed to seep through the papered walls.

He guided Ruzzo to a high-backed chair. The thing looked like it had been hand-carved when Abraham Lincoln was still in office. He dropped down, squirming like a schoolboy on the first day of class.

"You mind if I sit on the couch instead? It looks a little more com—"

The biker responded with a teeth-rattling backhand, almost knocking Ruzzo to the ground.

"Shut your trap."

Ruzzo righted himself, bringing a hand up to check for blood.

"That's enough...for now."

They both looked over to the base of the sweeping staircase. A thickset man was standing there in blue satin pajamas. Tufts of brown hair clung to the sides of his big, bald head.

He strolled forward as the biker stomped out of the room.

"I feel like I owe you an apology."

Ruzzo leaned back, trying to regain his composure.

"No need. I've been hit harder than that."

The man laughed, sitting down on the couch opposite him.

"Oh, I'm not sorry about some little love tap. There's plenty more where that came from. I'm more concerned about whatever lies led you to our little town."

"There must be some misunderstanding. I'm looking for a friend of mine."

"Yes, I know. Shayna Billups, if I'm not mistaken. That's why I sent my men over to find you."

Ruzzo winced. *I'll have to pay that motel clerk a visit if I ever make it out of here alive.*

He made a show of letting his eyes wander around the ornately decorated room. It didn't look like any biker den he'd seen before.

"Nice place you've got here. I'm surprised you let those scumbags hang around."

"You'd be surprised how hard it is to maintain a home of this size. No different than running this town, in many ways."

"So, 'Mayor' isn't just a nickname?"

"It's about the only thing that people around here call me anymore. It's gotten to where I can barely remember my own name sometimes. It's Charlie Bones, by the way."

He stood up, holding out his right hand. Ruzzo leaned in to shake, getting cold-cocked by a left instead. The blow sent him and the chair backwards onto the enormous area rug. Ruzzo groaned and gritted his teeth. He wanted nothing more than to snap The Mayor's neck, but knew he wouldn't make it out of there alive.

His hair was only inches from the fire when The Mayor yanked him up by his shirt.

"I'm as friendly as the next guy, except when somebody comes around looking for trouble."

He made Ruzzo pick up the chair and sit again. The Mayor's eyes caught the fire as he placed his hands on Ruzzo's shoulders.

"The person you're looking for isn't in Stone-haven any longer."

"If she's even alive."

The Mayor cocked his big, round head to the left an inch. His concerned look only lasted a second.

"My guess is she's probably gone back down where she belongs."

"You mean Florida, or the bottom of the ocean?"

"Point is, she isn't here."

He released Ruzzo, taking a step back.

"I suggest you follow behind her if you know what's good for you. I'll give you twenty-four hours."

The bikers reappeared as The Mayor labored up the stairs and disappeared. They had a third man with them now. He was smaller than the other two and dressed more like a preppy college professor than some wannabe Hells Angel.

Ruzzo stood up to head for the front door. One of the bigger men threw a shoulder into his as he passed. Ruzzo was already achy from his tumble to the floor, but wasn't about to let it show. He let the blow push him into the smaller man. They were eye-to-eye as he passed. There was something there that Ruzzo didn't see in the other men, a sharpness that made him seem even more out of place.

The biggest of the three bikers flashed a yellow smile while pushing Ruzzo outside.

"Welcome to Stonehaven."

CANNON POWDER

Ruzzo woke Mikey up the minute he got back to the motel. He wanted to splash cold water on his friend's face, like Sgt. Badeaux had done to him, but the half-empty beer on the nightstand was closer.

Mikey screamed, throwing wild punches before his eyes were even open.

"I'll shit down your neck!"

Ruzzo managed to sidestep the blind volley by an inch or two.

"Get cleaned up. The clock's ticking."

Mikey seemed to calm down at the sound of Ruzzo's voice. He wiped the warm beer from his eyes, licking his lips.

"What the hell's going on?"

"I had a little run in with the local goon squad while you were getting your beauty rest. They gave us until tomorrow morning to get out of town."

A confused look spread across Mikey's bloated face.

"Does that mean you found Shayna?"

Ruzzo chose his words carefully, but they got caught in his throat.

"A lot of people around here seem to think she's dead."

Mikey threw an arm around Ruzzo's shoulder, pulling him into a bear hug.

"You believe them?"

"Doesn't matter what I believe. I need to know for sure."

Mikey gave him a slap on the back.

"Well, *I need* to take a dump."

Mikey shuffled off to the bathroom. Ruzzo went back to his room to clean up and grab his gun. They agreed to meet down in the lobby in fifteen minutes. Ruzzo arrived early and immediately started dinging the bell on the counter.

The same clerk from the previous night lumbered into view a minute later. He was stretching and scratching like he'd recently woken up. His eyelids were still heavy with sleep, but went wide when he recognized Ruzzo. The clerk's recovery was feeble at best.

"Checking out so soon?"

Ruzzo had no time to waste. He looked around to make sure they were alone before lifting his shirt to expose the gun tucked into the front of his pants.

The clerk brought his hands up, as if he was being robbed.

Ruzzo snapped at him.

"Stop that! Act normal."

The clerk did as he was told. Ruzzo noticed his hands were trembling now.

"I met a friend of yours last night."

"You have to understand. I didn't have a choice."

"I get it, but now you're going to make it up to me. Where should I start looking for Shayna."

"I have no idea. Like I said, I—"

Ruzzo pulled the gun out, but left it dangling at his side. They were locked in a staring contest when Mikey came crashing through the lobby door. He went straight over to the continental breakfast buffet to pour himself a cup of coffee. Ruzzo coughed to get his attention.

Mikey looked up over the rim of his Styrofoam cup.

"Is this the guy you were telling me about?"

"No, but he's the one that tipped him off."

Ruzzo turned back to the clerk.

"Ain't that right?"

"Please, don't shoot. He pays me to keep an eye on things for him. He pays half the town!"

Mikey came up right behind Ruzzo, doing his

best to look threatening. He smelled like cheap soap and fresh vomit. Ruzzo pushed him back a few inches while addressing the clerk.

"Last chance. I need to find out what happened to Shayna."

The man's voice trembled now, too.

"The pirates, down by the river."

Ruzzo couldn't imagine that there were more than a few Captain Aurora impersonators in town, even in a tourist trap like this.

"Which one?"

"Any one of them. Ask for the cannon powder."

They left the motel, heading downtown on foot. Mikey was huffing and puffing as he tried to keep up with Ruzzo.

"What's the plan? We trying to score blow from every pirate we see?"

"Unless you've got any other bright ideas."

The first pirate they encountered was well past his prime. The buttons on his shirt strained against a bulging gut, and his beard was more nicotine yellow than blond. His decaying smile was incredibly accurate by seventeenth century standards.

"Ahoy! Care for a picture with Captain Aurora?"

He was talking to Ruzzo, but Mikey stepped in to answer.

"We were actually looking for something else."

Mikey tapped the side of his nose with an index finger. The pirate arched an eyebrow, nodding to a couple of younger pirates a hundred yards away. Both men looked up when Ruzzo and Mikey approached. Ruzzo did the talking this time, although he didn't have much to say.

"Cannon powder."

The shorter of the two men swiveled his head to survey their surroundings. His wide eyes were dull and pronounced gaps separated his teeth. Ruzzo thought he looked more like a caveman in a puffy shirt than a pirate.

His partner took a step closer to Ruzzo. He was doing a passable Keith Richards impression. This fancier pirate twisted his lips into a mock slur, rolling his shoulders and cocking his head as he spoke.

"You a cop?"

"No, but I've got a gun."

The pirate leaned in to mock him.

"Prove it, tough guy."

"Come any closer and I'll show you one of the bullets."

Caveman Pirate heard what was happening and tried to bolt. Mikey grabbed him by the ponytail, almost yanking him to the ground. He pulled him up at the last second instead, throwing an arm around the man's narrow shoulders as though they were old friends.

Fancy Pirate transformed into a statue on the spot. Ruzzo knew he didn't need to repeat himself, but did so anyway.

"Cannon powder."

"I-I-I—"

"Spit it out."

"In my pocket. Please don't take it all. He'll kill me."

"Who? The Mayor?"

Both pirates cringed at the mention of their new boss's name. Ruzzo knew they were on the right track.

"You can keep all of it. I'm looking for some information about a friend of mine. Her name's Shayna Billups."

The pirates exchanged a glance. All eyes quickly shifted to Ruzzo, including Mikey's. Ruzzo waited for Fancy Pirate to speak up. It took a moment, but the man's words rocked Ruzzo back on his heels.

"The last time I saw her alive was out on Corcoran Island. That was maybe a week ago. The night they sank Aurora's Galley."

"You were there?"

"Hell, yes, I was. We were both part of her crew."

"Okay. Thanks."

Ruzzo turned to walk away, but Fancy Pirate grabbed his shoulder.

"Wait. We want to come with you."

Ruzzo was skeptical at best.

"Why?"

"For revenge."

The Corcoran Island ferry looked more like a tugboat than a frigate. Throngs of tourists milled among the cars on the deck, leaning against the rail to take in the view. A few of them began asking for pictures with the two pirates standing between Ruzzo and Mikey. The impersonators happily obliged, collecting their usual fees as if nothing out of the ordinary was happening.

The boat was pulling up to the dock when the last of the tourists wandered off. Ruzzo was feeling sleep-deprived as they went to rent a golf cart. The four of them piled in and they puttered off. Ruzzo felt like he was working at Precious Acres retirement community in Seatown again, and it made him want to puke.

He was behind the wheel, with Mikey in the passenger seat. The pirates were in the back, telling them which way to go. Or, at least, Fancy Pirate was. Caveman Pirate might as well have had his tongue cut out for as little talking as he did.

"The field isn't too far from here."

Ruzzo made eye contact with them in the rearview mirror.

"And that's the last place you saw her?"

Both pirates nodded in unison. Ruzzo really wanted them to change out of their costumes, but the only thing for sale on the ferry were Captain Aurora T-shirts. He decided that two pirates in matching pirate T-shirts would only make them more conspicuous. The whole situation was a little too ridiculous for Ruzzo to wrap his head around.

They cruised along the smooth concrete road for a mile or two before the pirates told them to stop.

"It's right over there, somewhere."

"Are you sure?"

"Not exactly. It was the middle of the night the last time we were here, and some bikers were trying to kill us."

A small, single-engine airplane glided in over-head as Ruzzo cranked the wheel to the left. They bounced along on the uneven ground for half a mile before reaching an open expanse of grass. He stepped on the pedal, heading straight for the middle.

It didn't take them long to find the hastily

covered grave. Ruzzo climbed out of the golf cart and went over to investigate. The loose dirt had been covered with rocks and tree branches, but it stood out in the otherwise empty field. He was disgusted that the local police were spending so much time looking for bodies on the sunken boat when this one was practically in plain sight. *Then again*, he thought. *I've been disappointed by small-town police work before.*

His eyes were on the evidence at his feet when the pirates walked up. A foul question sat on the tip of his tongue like a tiny ball of shit.

"You sure she isn't down there with the other pirate?"

"Absolutely positive. We're the ones that covered him up."

The last few words brought tears to Fancy Pirate's eyes. It was enough to shake Ruzzo out of his own head, at least for a moment.

"I'm sorry. I guess he was a friend of yours, huh?"

"He was. A good friend, but then I guess Edward was, too."

"Edward?"

"He's the one who sold Shayna out to The Mayor. He sold us all out."

There was something about the way those

pirates spoke about Shayna that made Ruzzo suspicious. He could feel the jealous rage rising up inside of him as he stepped away to catch his breath. They'd been sleeping with her, he was sure of it.

Mikey could see that his friend was struggling with something.

"You doing all right?"

"Why the hell would Shayna be out here looking for pirate treasure?"

Ruzzo looked up, his eyes coming to rest on the crossed palm trees instead. He slapped Fancy Pirate on the shoulder.

"What's over there?"

"I have no idea. Shayna asked the same thing that night we were out here digging."

Ruzzo jogged back over to the golf cart. He barely waited for the others to climb in before speeding off in the direction of the palm trees. The small airplane they had seen earlier was taking off again when they plowed through the trees at the far end of the runway. There was a delivery van parked in front of a hanger. Two men locked up the building's doors before climbing into their vehicle. Ruzzo waited until they drove off before he and the others made their way down there on foot.

There was an eerie stillness to the place when

they arrived. Ruzzo checked the locks on the hanger doors while Mikey and the pirates walked the perimeter of the building.

Mikey grabbed a big rock to break one of the windows, but Ruzzo stopped him. He pointed to an alarm sign hanging on the wall.

"We don't need any visitors. They'll be on The Mayor's payroll."

"Better to know than to keep guessing."

Ruzzo's shoulders tensed up. His fists were tight balls. He became acutely aware that he hadn't eaten or slept for too many hours.

"There has to be another way in."

Mikey dropped the rock, clapping his hands to get the dust off. The pirates were already walking down the runway to get back into the golf cart.

"Let's do one more lap, just to be sure."

"Whatever you say, bubba."

Ruzzo circled the hangar clockwise while Mikey went in the opposite direction. They called out Shayna's name as they walked, louder each time. Neither of them had anything to report when they met around the back of the building a minute later.

Ruzzo's last shout was still ringing out when they both heard something. It was faint and sounded far away, but it was unmistakable. Somebody else was shouting Shayna's name too. They ran around to the front of the building to see if it was the two pirates, but they were still walking away in the wrong direction. The sound they'd heard was coming from the other end of the runway.

Ruzzo whirled around, screaming her name again.

"Shayna!"

The voice that came back was too high and pronounced to be an echo. He turned to Mikey, tossing him the keys.

"I'm heading down there. Get the golf cart and come find me."

Mikey's footsteps thundered off in the distance while Ruzzo tore down the runway screaming. And every time he heard it again, a little clearer with each step he took. It sounded like a child's voice now. Like they were playing some desperate, demented game of Marco Polo.

He was running at full tilt when he left the concrete and bounded into the woods. His voice was hoarse and raspy, so raw that he could almost taste blood in his throat.

"Shayna!"

The high-pitched voice was perfectly clear this time, and right overhead. Ruzzo looked up in time for a giant green parrot to shit in his eye. He was wiping the brown-and-white feces away when the bird took off in flight. It landed on an oak branch a little deeper in, where the shade made it harder to see. He called out Shayna's name once more, waiting for the response. The parrot's tone was pure mockery as it flapped away again.

Ruzzo took off at a sprint, his gut jiggling beneath him. He didn't actually think that this bird would lead him to Shayna, but it was the best lead he had at the moment. *Or maybe I've finally snapped.*

His lungs burned as he huffed and puffed under the strain of his own weight. He was soaked in sweat and getting delirious, but nothing could keep him from moving forward. The tree trunks seemed to jump out at him as he stumbled and tripped through the undergrowth. There were moments when he completely lost sight of the cursed bird, but all he had to do was call out her name again.

His rubbery legs felt like they were made of fire when the trees finally started to thin, revealing a sloping grass hill. He watched the bird glide effortlessly toward a two-story bungalow that rose up from the ground like an oasis. Ruzzo tripped and tumbled his way forward until he was crawling toward the small, sun-faded porch.

He rolled onto his back to look up. The parrot

was perched on the railing of a second floor balcony. The late morning sun was directly overhead, shining down on him like an unwanted spotlight. He managed to croak out her name one last time, lifting a hand to shield his shit-encrusted eyes. The electric blue sky felt like it was caving in on him when he heard the response. It sounded familiar, but it wasn't the parrot this time. And it wasn't saying "Shayna" either.

The voice was calling out his name.

"Tommy?! Oh my God, I knew you'd find me, Little Bear!"

A blurry silhouette slowly transformed into familiar curves. Details filled in little by little, until he was sure that it really was Shayna. She was wearing a small bikini top and waving a feather duster at him. A warm sense of relief spread throughout his entire body. A smile tugged at his lips as exhaustion and euphoria finally overwhelmed him. Everything went black.

BATTEN DOWN THE HATCHES

Ruzzo tried to sit up, but his body felt like a bag of wet sand. A TV was on somewhere nearby, mingling with the distant voices of Mikey and the pirates. And there was a repetitive clicking sound too. He opened his eyes to see the green parrot up on its perch. It had one eye on Ruzzo while pecking at a small wooden block that hung from a rope.

Ruzzo turned his head to the side. A very old man was seated in a recliner with his feet up. His hair was solid white, but his drawn face was beet red. He wore khaki pants and a light blue sweater that perfectly matched his argyle socks. His impossibly thin body looked like it was disintergrating into the puffy leather cushions engulfing him.

His eyes were open wide and fixed on something on the opposite wall. Ruzzo followed the man's gaze, expecting to see the TV, but found Shayna instead. She was facing the wall, playfully dusting the family picture frames hanging there. Ruzzo could see now that the bottom of her bikini was a thong.

Ruzzo called out to her, but his voice was a soft growl. In the end, it was the parrot that got her attention. Shayna turned around at the sound of her name, practically fluttering across the room to smother him in kisses. She was sitting beside him with tears in her eyes.

"I was so worried about you."

He could only manage a smile. She brought her hand up to stroke his cheek.

"What are these bruises on your face from?"

His shattered voice could only produce a few words at a time.

"Battle wounds."

Shayna frowned, but didn't miss a beat.

"Mikey's in the kitchen with my crew. Want me to get him for you?"

"Not yet."

Ruzzo set a hand down on her knee.

"Seatown isn't the same without you."

"Well, you're here with me now."

Shayna stood up and went into the kitchen. Ruzzo's heart ached as she walked away.

There was a glass of water in her hand when she finally returned. She brought it to his lips, letting him take a few small sips. The icy liquid burned his throat going down, but his thirst overcame the pain. He took the glass from her, drinking it down in a couple of gulps. She got up to refill it when he finished, but Ruzzo grabbed her wrist.

"What are you doing here?"

She sat back down, brushing the hair from his forehead.

"It's complicated."

"I'm not going anywhere."

Shayna tilted her head to search his eyes.

"You seem different."

"I got fat. Florida does that to New Yorkers."

"That's not what I'm talking about. I love the way you look, but you're a little more intense. And you were pretty intense in the first place."

"It's been a tough year."

"Well, it's kind of turning me on."

She snuck a glance over her shoulder to where the old man was sitting. He was fast asleep. Shayna giggled while rubbing circles on his chest with the palm of her hand.

"Why don't you come upstairs with me and I'll tell you all about it?"

It could have been the water, or it could have been the way that she smelled sitting so close to him, but Ruzzo didn't have any trouble standing up this time.

✳ ✳ ✳

Shayna slid off of him with a satisfied sigh. Ruzzo's mind had been blank a moment before, but now it was flooding with questions. He rolled onto his side and gave her a kiss on the cheek.

"You want to tell me who the old man is downstairs?"

She turned to kiss him on the lips. Her breath smelled like sweet coffee.

"He's my boss. Jealous?"

"You were putting on quite a show for the old pervert."

"Be nice. His name's Mr. Nelson, and he saved my life."

Ruzzo laughed for the first time in too long.

"He's barely saving his own life these days."

"Well, he took me in when I was stranded and desperate. My body was the only thing I had to offer in trade."

Ruzzo grimaced while Shayna went on.

"But don't get any ideas. He's so old that a little blue pill couldn't even help him get it up. He likes to watch me work."

"That makes two of us."

She reached up to pinch his nipple, hard. He was waving the white flag before she even let go.

"Okay, okay. So you've been hiding out here?"

"A little hiding and a lot of planning. When I'm not cleaning the house, that is."

Shayna flashed an evil grin. Ruzzo knew he was in trouble.

"Tell me more about these plans of yours."

"I'm guessing you've met The Mayor by now."

"He's a hard guy to miss around here. Especially when he sends his goons to fetch you in the middle of the night."

Shayna sat up, resting her arms on bent knees. Ruzzo studied the soft curves on her hips and legs, and the muscly arc of her back. Concern was written all over Shayna's face when he met her eyes again.

"Oh, sweetie. Please tell me that isn't where you got these bruises."

"I won't lie to you. What'd you do to piss him off?"

"If you ask him, I came looking to steal his treasure."

"And if I ask you?"

"We can talk about that later. Right now I have some other plans on my mind."

"Aren't you afraid your boss will catch you screwing around on the clock?"

"I do have a little more cleaning to do..." She

slid her hand down under the sheets. "Now where did I leave that duster?"

Shayna was back in the bath again, only this one wasn't quite as luxurious. There were bulky aluminum handrails bolted to the wall to help the old man get in and out of the shower. And the tub itself was smaller by a foot or two than her claw foot, which meant she had to bend her knees to fit. To make matters worse, Ruzzo was snoring so loudly in the bedroom next door that the bathroom windows rattled.

None of that mattered. She had to lure The Mayor and his men back to the island, but that was only step one. There was no way that she and her skeleton crew of two would ever win against him in a fair fight, even with Ruzzo and Mikey on her side.

She slid down until her head was submerged, but kept her eyes open. Being surrounded by hot water always cleared her mind, turning the unnecessary thoughts to steam. She kept her body still, studying the blank white ceiling overhead. A couple of flies did loops around each other in the space between, a futile chase that would only end when one of them dropped dead.

She sat up in the tub, reaching for her towel on the floor. She had the answer she'd been searching for, the perfect way to steal the treasure and make it out of North Carolina alive.

Shayna stepped from the tub to dry off. She'd already killed a man who loved her once before. *The second time should be a piece of cake.*

Mikey and the pirates were already drunk when Shayna and Ruzzo came downstairs two hours later. It hadn't taken the three of them long to find the old man's liquor cabinet. It mostly consisted of odds and ends from the last thirty years. They'd already been through a bottle of rum he brought back from the Caribbean in the late eighties. A few ancient airline bottles of scotch were next on the agenda. A crusty bottle of Frangelico was in their sights after that.

It might have infuriated Ruzzo the day before, but for now he let it roll off his back. His quest to find Shayna was complete. Whatever came next would be a completely new adventure. He was hoping that this time somebody else would be in charge.

Shayna flung the refrigerator door open. She pulled out some tomatoes, garlic and Parmesan cheese, setting them down on butcher's block. The pasta was up in the cupboard along with the olive oil. She filled a stockpot with water and set it to boil on the stove. Ruzzo almost couldn't believe his eyes. He had never seen her cook before.

Once everything was assembled, she turned to Caveman Pirate.

"Make dinner, but keep listening while you cook. I think I found a way that we can still get that treasure."

Mikey, for one, was all ears. He hadn't heard much about the map or treasure since he and Ruzzo left New Orleans. It seemed like the proximity of two pirates made it real for him somehow, which was good. Shayna was going to need every man she could get to pull this off.

"The Mayor and his crew have been out here with Edward a few times since the night they sank Aurora's Galley."

Both pirates muttered obscenities at the mention of Edward's name. Ruzzo gave Shayna a questioning look. She couldn't ignore it, much as she would have liked to.

"Edward was part of our crew, but he betrayed us. He's working for The Mayor now."

Ruzzo heard something in her voice, something else that she wasn't telling him. He knew he'd have to wait to get a straight answer about Edward.

"They all think you're dead."

"That's right, and we need to keep it that way."

Shayna noticed that Mikey's glass was empty, so she refilled it for him. She did the same for the pirates before going on. Ruzzo took the opportunity to jump in again.

"I wouldn't mind staying off The Mayor's radar."

Shayna offered him a drink too, but he waved her off. This was the most clear-headed he'd been in a year. She smiled at him like a proud parent.

"We'll get to that in a minute. Now where was I?"

Fancy Pirate grunted the word "treasure."

"Oh, right. I heard a few of his men talking the last time they were out here."

Ruzzo's concern for Shayna overwhelmed him.

"What do you mean you 'overheard' them? Please tell me you weren't close enough to hear their entire conversation."

"This island's so quiet at night that you can hear teenagers screwing on the beach all the way over in Stonehaven. And those bikers talk pretty loud when they don't think anybody's listening."

Ruzzo thought back to his first night at the hotel and wondered if they were walking into another trap. He bit his tongue and listened while Shayna went on.

"They haven't found anything yet, but it sounds like they're getting really close. One of them mentioned that they were about to get some more information. He said they might be coming back late on Saturday night to finish the job."

Ruzzo couldn't bite his tongue any longer. The cop in him refused to believe there was anything real about this local legend.

"I know I'm still new to this treasure hunt, but do you really think that Captain Aurora left something buried out here?"

Caveman Pirate snorted. Fancy Pirate slapped the table with the palm of his hand.

"Of course there's treasure out here. That's all we've been hearing about since elementary school."

Shayna let them finish, nodding along in agreement.

"I held the map in my hand, Tommy. It's real."

Ruzzo was still skeptical, but knew he would end up doing whatever Shayna wanted him to. There was no point in coming this far only to let her down. He nodded to Mikey for a second opinion.

"What do you think?"

Mikey raised his glass in a toast.

"Sounds more fun than being a bartender. Tell me more."

Shayna told them everything, including how she planned to steal the treasure from The Mayor and his men once they'd dug it up. She turned to Ruzzo after laying out her detailed plan. There was only one part she'd left out.

"The first thing we need to do is send you back into Stonehaven, where The Mayor can see you."

Ruzzo stood up and started pacing.

"Why can't we wait until they show up out here this weekend? That's only two days from now."

"He probably already thinks you're part of the plan to steal his treasure. It'll force him to make his move faster if he knows you're still snooping around."

"I don't know…"

"Come on, baby. You'll look great dressed as a pirate."

BLACK SPOT

Ruzzo and Mikey stood on the dock, adjusting their fake beards. They wore matching sashes and headscarves, plastic knives shoved into the waist of their pantaloons. It was the same collection of props that most of the other impersonators used, but Ruzzo had something in his pocket that was very real. Shayna had given it to him right before they left. She told him only to share it with The Mayor.

They were near where the Aurora used to be moored. It was a big, empty space now, with a sign and a ramp that led nowhere. They'd only been there for a few minutes, but several tourists had already approached them looking for "cannon powder."

Mikey did most of the talking. Unfortunately, his pirate accent sounded like a drunk Australian trying to do a Richard Nixon impression. He so badly butchered the few pirate phrases Shayna's men had taught him that it was only making matters worse. Most conversations ended with him scowling

"Arrgggghhhhh" repeatedly until the tourists fled, fearing for their lives.

The mission to make a spectacle of themselves was working exactly according to Shayna's plan. It didn't take long for a couple of The Mayor's men to roll up on their motorcycles. Ruzzo recognized them as the two bikers he'd followed out of the motel the previous night. He was ready for them when they lumbered over.

"Well, if it isn't Tweedle Dum and Tweedle Idiot."

The look on the tall one's face was half smile, half sneer. His partner wore a pinched expression as he stared Ruzzo down.

"What are you two sissies up to?"

Ruzzo gave an exaggerated glance to his right and left. Pirate impersonators of all sizes were scattered along the waterfront as far as the eye could see. He turned back to the bikers, leaning in to whisper.

"I think you've got me confused with one of your other boyfriends."

The smaller biker tried to throw a punch, but his buddy stuck an arm out to hold him back. Mikey took a step forward. Things were getting tense fast, so Ruzzo started asking more questions.

"You guys come all the way out here to tell me

that I look familiar to you? Because we just met last night."

"The Mayor wanted us to remind you that your twenty-four hours are up."

Ruzzo delivered the line he'd been practicing in his head all afternoon.

"About that. We did a little *digging* on The Mayor. Seems like he might be hiding something that we wouldn't mind finding ourselves."

The big biker shook his head, acting heartbroken over what he had to do next. He made a fist with his right hand, cracking his knuckles with the palm of his left. Mikey whipped Ruzzo's gun out and brought the tip of the barrel to rest on the man's forehead. Both bikers froze.

Now it was Mikey's turn to recite his lines.

"Tell The Mayor that we have a copy of the map. He can either buy it from us, or we'll sell it to the highest bidder."

A smile was smeared across Ruzzo's face now. He wasn't trying to hide it at all.

"Tell The Mayor he has twenty-four hours."

The bikers backed away slowly. They looked more annoyed than scared.

"You punks better watch yourselves. He don't take kindly to threats."

"Do we look scared?"

The bikers traded worried looks while Ruzzo pressed on.

"You think you two idiots can remember all that, or should I write it down for you?"

"Come with us. You can tell him yourself."

Heads turned as they rode through town to The Mayor's house. Ruzzo was sweating bullets since he'd always thought of motorcycles as two-wheeled death machines. He looked to his left and saw Mikey there on the bike beside him, leaning back and enjoying the ride. *It's a good thing the boys back at the NYPD can't see me now.*

They wove through the side streets and into The Mayor's driveway. The place looked even bigger in the light of day. Ruzzo noticed a squadron of gardeners spread out around the property as he climbed off the motorcycle. Mikey had the gun out again as they walked over to the porch, but Ruzzo told him to put it away.

"He won't shoot us in his own house in broad daylight. There are too many witnesses around."

"How can you be so sure?"

"Half the town saw us coming over here. We were kind of hard to miss."

The bikers led them inside, heading straight for

the living room.

"Wait here while we go find The Mayor."

Ruzzo saw the high-backed wooden chair he'd sat in last time, but opted for the couch instead. He didn't want to relive any unpleasant memories unless it was absolutely necessary. There was no roaring fire or classical music this time, probably because The Mayor hadn't been expecting guests.

Mikey wandered around the room studying the historical knick-knacks on display. There was a small pirate's ship in a glass bottle, a hand-painted coffee mug in the shape of a pirate's head, an unused glass ashtray emblazoned with the image of a gold doubloon, and a wooden box that held a brass telescope. He was thumbing through a Captain Aurora coffee-table book when somebody walked in. Ruzzo recognized him as the preppy college professor he'd seen on his way out of this same room the night before.

Ruzzo stood up, ready to fight.

"I'm only willing to deal with The Mayor."

The man took a step forward, holding out his hand.

"The name's Edward. I believe we have a friend in common."

Ruzzo rose up, resisting the urge to head butt him. If there was one thing he hated it was a traitor, but that wasn't all. There was something about this Edward character—his knowing smile, and the cocksure tone of his voice—that filled Ruzzo with that familiar jealous rage. He could practically smell Shayna all over this Benedict Arnold.

"She's no friend of yours."

"I suppose that's true given the circumstances, but don't judge me too harshly. The situation is more complicated than you're probably aware."

"Whatever. Where's The Mayor?"

"Indisposed, I'm afraid. He asked me to come speak with you. How is Shayna, by the way? Did she ask you to tell me anything?"

Ruzzo wanted to knock the smug look right off the bastard's face, but sat down on the sofa instead. He needed to remind himself that they were there on a mission.

"We haven't been able to find her."

Ruzzo looked over at Mikey who was right beside him now, cleaning his nails with a Captain Aurora letter opener shaped like a cutlass. Edward took a seat opposite them.

"Okay, then, let's get down to it. My men tell me that you claim to have a copy of our map. I know for certain that it isn't true. If there was a copy, I'm the one who would have made it."

Edward leaned back, crossing his legs. Ruzzo leaned forward across the coffee table. He wasn't about to get outsmarted by some two-bit actor.

"If that's your story, then fine. As long as you're willing to explain that to your boss when we take the treasure. I guess this conversation is over."

Ruzzo and Mikey stood up. They were headed for the front door when a voice rang out from the top of the stairs.

"You know there isn't any treasure, right?"

Ruzzo spun around to look up at The Mayor. He was wearing an ill-fitting golf shirt tucked into too-tight khaki pants. The pork pie hat looked a few sizes too small on his humongous head.

"The map must be worth something if you're willng to kill for it. Besides, we already have proof that the treasure exists."

The Mayor took a few steps down the staircase, but stopped on the landing. He turned to the wall, adjusting a framed picture hanging there.

"It's a family heirloom. The value is purely sentimental, but I'm willing to humor you. How much for this imaginary duplicate of the map?"

"Fifty thousand."

The Mayor finished his descent.

"If that's the price, I'll need to see this proof of yours."

Ruzzo tossed him the small gem he'd been carrying in his pocket all day. A thin film of sweat began to form on The Mayor's upper lip, despite the cool air inside the house. Something about that stone completely shattered his calm exterior.

"Where did you get this?"

"We dug it up last night, along with a few others just like it. Won't be long before we uncover the whole thing."

The Mayor took a deep breath, trying to regain his composure. Ruzzo watched as he transformed back into the powerful man he was, like a chameleon changing colors.

"Very interesting." There was a renewed fire in his gaze as his eyes shifted back to Ruzzo's. "But what's stopping me from killing you right now?"

"That would be unfortunate since there are other parties already interested in our copy of the map. If my partners don't hear from me in the next fifteen minutes, it goes to the highest bidder."

The Mayor tossed the gem back to Ruzzo. It obviously pained him to give it back.

"Let's say that I was willing to pay that ridiculous ransom. How would you prefer I deliver the cash?"

"Corcoran Island. Tomorrow night."

"Will Shayna be with you?"

Ruzzo narrowed his eyes.

"Rumor has it you killed her."

The Mayor shoved his hands in his pockets, rocking forward on the balls of his feet. His eyes darted from Ruzzo to Mikey while he considered their offer.

"As luck would have it, I was planning to be out there tomorrow evening any way. Would eight o'clock work?"

"We'll meet you in the field by the airport, but we won't wait long."

"I'll make this easy for you. If we're not there by eight, we aren't coming at all."

The Mayor started up the stairs, barking out orders as he went.

"Edward, get these assholes out of my house. Right now."

Edward escorted them out onto the front porch and down the long driveway. The two bikers were lounging on their motorcycles, clearly disappointed to see their guests leaving in one piece. Edward didn't say another word until they reached the sidewalk, completely out of earshot of the others.

"Tell Shayna that I'll make sure The Mayor is there, with the cash."

This wasn't something that Shayna had prepared him for. Ruzzo tried to play it cool, but he wasn't much of an actor. In the end he decided it was best to keep it simple.

"Shayna's dead."

They were at the ferry terminal before Mikey finally asked the question that had been eating at him since leaving The Mayor's house.

"What was that all about?"

"Hell if I know. Let's get back out to the island and ask Shayna."

If Seatown was quiet compared to New York, Corcoran Island was practically a morgue. Ruzzo listened to the clicking sound the mosquitos made as they banged against the bedroom window, trying desperately to get inside. He could hear the crickets outside, too, each chirp a little more unnerving than the last. Every little sound made him long for the nonstop white noise of Queens, the traffic, the trains and the two a.m. gunshots.

Shayna slipped back into the room, dropping her robe as she walked. Ruzzo knew that it wouldn't be quiet much longer.

"How's the old man?"

"Sleeping, finally. I swear sometimes he thinks I'm his dead wife."

She stopped at the vanity to check her hair in the

mirror. Ruzzo couldn't wait to get his hands on that body again.

"It's going to be a mess in a minute."

Shayna turned around with a smile, but Ruzzo's eyes were elsewhere. She let him enjoy the view, using the distance between them as foreplay.

"I don't make myself pretty for you, silly. I do it for me."

"Well, whatever you're doing, it's working."

Ruzzo flung the covers back, patting her side of the bed.

"Did you really dig that gem up out here?"

"I didn't dig it up, but it came from this island."

"That's pretty cryptic. Mind sharing a few details?"

"I'll tell you the whole story after we get our money tomorrow night."

Shayna sauntered forward a few steps, but stopped short of climbing in. She wore a strange expression that Ruzzo had never seen before.

"Why did you come looking for me?"

"I didn't have a choice. I can't stand to be away from you."

The words came out of his mouth before he even knew what they were. He could tell from her smile that he had said the right thing. His follow-up question shocked both of them.

"Who's Edward?"

Shayna lowered herself down to the edge of the bed, looking over her shoulder at him. It would normally be too tempting a sight for Ruzzo to ignore, but he forced himself to keep his eyes on hers.

She bit her lip, considering her answer carefully.

"A poor substitute for you."

"Do you love him?"

Ruzzo rushed his words, needing to get the bitter taste of them out his mouth. She leaned back, her head coming to rest on a pillow. They lay there side by side for a minute or two, neither of them speaking. The sound of the mosquitos and the crickets rose up again in the stillness, but Ruzzo was only paying attention to her breathing.

Shayna let out a soft sigh, rolling over to face him.

"What would you do if you could start all over?"

Ruzzo was starting to think she would never answer his question.

"From scratch? Like witness protection, or something?"

"Exactly. Totally erase yourself, like none of it ever happened."

Ruzzo tried to come up with something that would impress her, but his mind was blank. The only thing he wanted in life was already right next to him. Ruzzo wished he had a ring on him so that he could propose and get it over with.

"I want to be wherever you are."

Shayna planted a kiss on his cheek. She worked her way up to whisper in his ear.

"I can make you disappear, Tommy. We can start all over again. Trust me."

He closed his eyes, feeling the warmth of her breath on his neck.

"What about you?"

"I'm already dead, at least according to everybody in this town."

Ruzzo couldn't help but smile. Shayna always was a few steps ahead of him. *She would have made a great detective, if she didn't like breaking the law so much.*

"I do trust you…"

"Good, because the answer's yes."

Ruzzo pulled his head back an inch, his worst fears realized.

"You do love him?"

She brought a hand up to his chest.

"Yes, I'll marry you."

NO QUARTER

Ruzzo felt like a new man when he woke up the next morning. All of the self-hatred and self-doubt that had been eating him alive were suddenly gone. It was like a weight had been lifted from his chest, allowing him to breathe again for the first time in a year. He rolled over to wrap an arm around his new fiancée, but her side of the bed was empty. The sheets were cold and Shayna was gone.

He sat up in a panic, searching the room through squinted eyes. The windows were open and the curtains danced in a slight breeze, but there was no sign of her. Ruzzo swung his legs to the floor, standing up to stretch. He slipped into his boxers and T-shirt before opening the bedroom door.

The sound of Mikey's laughter greeted him when he got downstairs. He and Shayna were sitting at the kitchen table in the middle of an animated conversation. Ruzzo was shocked to see his friend sober for the first time in a week. He went over to pour himself a cup of coffee and sat down beside them.

Mikey raised his mug in a toast.

"I heard you're getting married. Congrats!"

Ruzzo glanced at Shayna, surprised she'd already shared the news. She beamed, resting her head on his shoulder. He eventually brought his mug up to clink it with Mikey's.

"Thanks. How do you feel about being my best man?"

"That would be amazing. I have some great stories for my speech."

The two pirates stumbled in a moment later. Unlike Mikey, they looked as if they were still drunk. Something about Shayna changed the minute they entered.

"You need to get yourselves fed and cleaned up. We have a lot of work to do."

"Yarrrrr, m'lady."

Shayna stood up, dropping her empty plate into the sink. It sounded like it might shatter. She gave Ruzzo a kiss on the top of the head on her way out of the room.

"You two come with me. I want to show you something."

Ruzzo and Mikey stood up. They walked through the living room where the old man was already asleep in his chair. Shayna was waiting for them on the porch when they got outside. She pointed up to the sky as a small airplane buzzed by overhead.

"That's how we're getting off the island once we get that treasure tonight."

Ruzzo frowned.

"Why can't we take a boat tomorrow morning?"

Shayna kept her eyes on the sky. Ruzzo could hear the guile in her voice.

"Because he'll never let us leave here alive."

"But none of us know how to fly."

She brought her chin down to look at Ruzzo. It was obvious that she had given this plan a lot more thought than he was giving her credit for.

"That's true, but I know somebody who does."

It was dark in the field that night. Ruzzo and Mikey were milling around near the grave, waiting for The Mayor and his men to show up. Fresh new holes dotted the landscape all around them, with shovels strewn around for good measure. Shayna and the pirates were hidden somewhere out of sight in the oak trees near the landing strip.

Ruzzo had half of their copy of the map, but Shayna had the other half. The plan went like this: Mikey was supposed to signal to Shayna with his flashlight once they had the cash. At that point, The

Mayor and his men would go over to complete the transaction with her. Shayna would, of course, be gone by the time they arrived.

Ruzzo liked the plan because it mostly kept his bride-to-be out of harm's way. It would have been perfect if it didn't end with them climbing into a small plane. He was still trying to think of ways around that when he heard voices on the edge of the field. Mikey must have heard it at the same time because he suddenly stood right beside him.

"Showtime."

"Stay cool. This will all be over soon, and then we can get on with our lives."

They could see The Mayor and his men coming through the trees. One of the bikers was waving a flashlight as they crossed the open space. The other two were waving guns, flanking The Mayor and making sure the coast was clear. They were about a hundred yards away when more voices came from further down the beach. Ruzzo turned to look, but it was too dark to make out who it was. He assumed it was another group of bikers bringing up the rear.

His attention turned back in the other direction when he heard The Mayor's voice.

"Let's get this over with. I've got other business to attend to."

The Mayor motioned to Edward. He stepped forward, popping the locks on a briefcase. Mikey jumped back an inch when the lid sprang open. Ruzzo bent over to look at the stacks of cash inside. His heart started racing as his head filled with second thoughts. *I might not be a cop any more, but that doesn't mean I'm a criminal.*

But Ruzzo knew that it was too late to walk away, and that he'd risk losing Shayna for good if he did. He took a deep breath, trying to collect himself. There was no turning back now. They'd already gone too far for that.

The Mayor must have seen the look on his face and decided to pounce.

"What's the matter? Getting cold feet. We can always call this whole thing off, if you give me your copy of the map. And the stone."

Ruzzo snatched a bundle of cash. He'd been on enough sting operations with the NYPD to fumble his way through this kind of negotiation. But for some reason, everything he thought to say sounded like a line from a bad gangster movie.

"All the cash better be there."

The Mayor must have seen the same movies, because he played right along.

"If I wanted to rip you off, I wouldn't have come all the way out here."

Ruzzo ran his thumb along the edge of the cash, riffling the stiff bills one by one. It sounded like he was shuffling a brand new deck of cards. Mikey nudged him with an elbow and nodded over his shoulder.

The other voices were much closer, and getting louder by the second. Ruzzo glanced in the direction of the noise, surprised to see two women and two men approaching. They were screaming at each other as they stumbled along in the gloom, making very slow progress. The one trailing furthest behind had a dark knit hat and flowing white beard that almost glowed in the darkness.

The Mayor heard them too, but kept his eyes on Ruzzo.

"What the hell is this?"

The two bikers stepped forward, raising their guns. Ruzzo held his half of the duplicate map up, shoving it into The Mayors hand. He threw the stack of cash back into the briefcase, slamming the lid shut. Edward didn't put up any resistance when Ruzzo yanked it away from him.

The Mayor lunged, grabbing Ruzzo by the collar.

"Hold on. Where's the other half of the map?"

"Shayna has it over there, in the trees."

Ruzzo pointed in the direction of the landing

strip. A small airplane flew overhead, as if on cue. Everybody looked up long enough for Mikey to grab the briefcase out of Ruzzo's hands. He ran as fast as his lumbering body allowed, tracing a jagged line as he went. The bikers fired at him as he ran for cover near the crossed palm trees. They chased after him once they realized they'd missed. Gunshots continued to erupt for a full minute after they all disappeared into the distance.

That left Ruzzo alone with The Mayor and Edward. Ruzzo took the opportunity to drive his fist straight into Edward's face. The sound of his nose shattering was like music to Ruzzo's ears. He sprang forward to throw a second punch when The Mayor wrapped a forearm around his neck.

"You better hope your friend's coming back with the second half of that map."

Ruzzo's face flushed as the flow of oxygen to his brain was cut off. He clawed at The Mayors arm, but couldn't pry it loose. His eyes bulged from his head as he watched the four strangers run up. Ruzzo finally recognized the man with the spiky hair as one of the junkies from New Orleans. He arrived at a gallop and didn't slow down before driving his fist into The Mayor's jaw.

The vicious blow sent Ruzzo spinning to the ground, while The Mayor stumbled backwards into a reverse somersault. He paid dearly for the slow recovery once Georgia and Ida arrived. The taller one pinned him down while the shorter one repeatedly kicked him in the ribs. There wasn't much fight left in him when Lafitte finally tottered up a minute later.

He walked straight up to Ruzzo, holding out a hand.

"Shayna said you'd be out here with my brother."

"He's your brother?"

Ruzzo looked over to where The Mayor was face down on the ground. Georgia, Ida and the bouncer backed off when Lafitte knelt down beside him.

"You'd never know judging by that big head of his. Ain't that right, Charlie?"

Lafitte rolled him over onto his back.

"I bet you were pretty surprised when Shayna showed up with that map."

The Mayor still wasn't responding, so Lafitte turned to Ruzzo for some answers.

"Were you there when he saw the stone? Did he shit himself?"

Ruzzo nodded like a confused child.

"I guess so—"

Lafitte started cackling. His laughter was identical to The Mayor's.

"I wish I could have been there to see that."

"I take it your name isn't really Lafitte."

"Nope. The locals down in New Orleans started calling me that when I opened that pirate bar. My real name's Dale Bones. I grew up out here on Corcoran Island with this loser."

The Mayor slowly came to life. He rolled onto his side, spitting a tooth into the dirt. Lafitte gave him a pat on the shoulder, muttering "there, there."

"Our dad was the one who originally found that map. Moved us all the way up here from Louisiana to dig for Captain Aurora's treasure. Of course, the only thing he ever claimed to have found was that one little gem. He usually kept it in his pocket, so my brother thought it was buried out here with our old man. But I had it with me in New Orleans this whole time."

Ruzzo tried to imagine what it was like to be raised by a treasure hunter. *It's no wonder both of his kids grew up addicted to pirates.*

"Your father's buried out here?"

"Right here in this field. We covered him up ourselves after Charlie killed him."

The Mayor lifted himself up onto an elbow. It sounded like his jaw might be broken from the way he slurred his words.

"It was an accident."

Lafitte gave a loud snort in response.

"You've been saying that for years, but it ain't the truth. You were the only one with him when he finally found that treasure. You got greedy, is all."

Ruzzo still couldn't believe what he was hearing.

"You're telling me the treasure is real?"

"Oh, it's real all right. Problem is, my idiot brother's the only one who knows where to find it."

"But the map says—"

"The crossed bones on that map is where *Captain Aurora* buried the treasure, but Charlie moved it the night he shot our dear old dad. He's refused to tell me where it is ever since. Ain't that right?"

The Mayor groaned while his brother went on.

"I tried for years to send somebody up here with that map and stone, but nobody took me up on it. People down in New Orleans got to thinking I was a nut job, going on and on about pirate treasure. And then Shayna walked through the door at Keely's and I knew I had my mark. Charlie always had a thing for crazy women with big knockers, so I guessed she'd get his attention. Looks like I was right."

The Mayor managed to get into a sitting position. It didn't look like he had any interest in standing up.

"That treasure's soaked in our father's blood. It needs to stay buried, just like him."

Three gunshots rang out from the direction of the landing strip, followed by the sound of Shayna screaming. They all swung their heads to look, but it was too dark and too far away to see anything.

Edward leapt up and started running. Ruzzo was a few steps behind him.

Edward already had his arms draped around Shayna when Ruzzo ran up. They were standing on the landing strip a few feet from a small airplane. The two bikers were on the ground at their feet, both of them missing half of their heads. The look on Mikey's face told the whole story.

Ruzzo went over to take the gun from his shaking hand.

"It'll be all right. It was self-defense."

"How do you know? You weren't even here."

"I know you wouldn't have shot them otherwise."

The two pirates came around the front of the plane, shoving the pilot between them. He was a heavyset man with a thick, black mustache and hooded eyes. The word "Miami" was stitched across the front of his faded baseball cap.

Shayna grabbed the gun from Ruzzo's hand, shoving it into the pilot's face.

"Please don't shoot me. I'm only the courier!"

She kept the barrel pressed against the man's fat cheek, while addressing the pirates.

"They're about to dig up the treasure. You two should go over to the field and take whatever you can. It's all yours, anything you manage to grab for yourselves."

"But, m'lady. What about you and—?"

"Go! You've earned it."

The pirates looked at each other before releasing the pilot. Ruzzo could see the greed sparkling in their eyes as they took off down the landing strip. He waited until they were gone before he spoke up.

"You're just going to let them have it, after all of your planning?"

"Don't worry. The Mayor would rather die than tell them where it is."

"Lafitte wouldn't kill his brother."

"If those psychos from New Orleans don't kill him, my pirates definitely will. I'd be surprised if any of them make it out alive. Buried gold makes people crazy."

Ruzzo was getting annoyed. He couldn't contain the anger in his voice.

"So then why the hell are we out here?"

"The treasure we're after isn't golden, it's white." Shayna took a step closer to the pilot, spitting out words as she leaned in. "How much cocaine is on the plane?"

"F-f-fifty kilos."

Ruzzo did the math in his head, coming up with a street value of one-point-five million. He guessed that Shayna already had that figured out. She turned to the pilot.

"You have enough gas on the plane to get the four us out of here?"

The pilot's eyes darted between them. He wasn't the only one who realized that there were five people standing there. There were only four seats on the plane.

Shayna suddenly spun, the barrel of the gun coming to rest a few inches from Edward's chest.

"I'm really sorry about this."

He brought both hands up, his voice a simpering whine.

"No, Shayna, don't. I did everything according to the plan. I got The Mayor out here for you, and…and…"

A single shot rang out. Edward clutched at the gaping wound in his chest as he crumpled to the ground. Ruzzo immediately went into cop mode.

He knelt beside Edward to stop the bleeding, but there was simply too much of it.

"Oh my God, Shayna! What did you do?"

She brought the gun down, trying to regain control of the situation.

"This is almost over, Tommy. We only have a few more things to do before we can disappear together."

"He's dead. What else is there left to do?"

"We need to put your I.D. in his pocket so the police will find it with his remains after we burn the hangar down. Make sure to put it in his metal wallet so it doesn't melt."

Shayna was calm as she handed him a small key. Ruzzo's voice was raspy and broken as he tried to wrap his head around her ever-changing plans.

"Nobody's going to believe that Edward is me. The Mayor will see right through this, and so will the local police."

"The police will have their hands full with the other bodies, including The Mayor's. I doubt they'll be too worried about Edward's charred bones. Besides, we'll be ghosts by then."

Ruzzo was stunned into silence. He was equally impressed and horrified by his fiancée.

Mikey stood there with a blank expression on his face. The pilot dropped down to his knees and started praying. Shayna pressed the gun against his temple.

"How far can you take us?"

"I'm supposed to fly back to Miami tonight, but this is a lot more weight."

"You think you can at least get us to the Florida Panhandle?"

The pilot stood up. He and Shayna climbed into the plane while Ruzzo and Mikey carried Edward's limp body over to the hangar. The place was dark and mostly empty, except for a van that was parked to the side. Shayna had already placed a pile of rags and a can of gasoline beside it. They dragged Edward, sliding him under the wheels. Ruzzo took the metal wallet from Edward's pocket and unlocked it. He swapped his license with Edward's, sticking it into his own pocket.

Mikey shoved a soaked rag into the gas tank of the vehicle. Ruzzo poured a trail of gasoline that extended across the oil-stained floor and out through the large sliding doors. The plane's engines roared to life behind them as Mikey dropped a match. They watched the line of fire race toward the van for a brief moment before turning to run.

A series of gunshots rang out in the distance as they jumped into the plane with the pilot and Shayna. Ruzzo wondered if any of them had survived out in that field, or if Captain Aurora managed to claim another handful of lives.

They were a few feet off the runway, gaining elevation, when the van exploded inside of the hangar. The shock waves made the plane dance a little as it rose up into the night sky.

MAROONED

Ruzzo had never been to the Caribbean before and was mesmerized by the white sand beaches and crystal clear water. And the sweaty tropical sex was good, too.

The lounge chair that Shayna was sitting on was only a few inches from his, just the way he liked it. He slid the sunglasses from his nose, trying to imagine what the island must have looked like back when pirates ruled. These days it was filled with international tourists sipping on overpriced rum drinks before boarding their cruise ships.

Shayna reached over to give his hand a squeeze.

"Where the hell's Mikey?"

"Up in his room changing. Don't worry, he's never late for dinner."

There was a fantastic seafood shack that they'd been to almost every night since arriving a week ago. A few of the local kids had a little reggae band that set up outside on the patio. They weren't great musicians, but what they lacked in talent they more than made up for with passion.

Shayna reached over to run her fingers through

his hair. He brought his cocktail up to take a drink. The sun was setting out across the sea as he said a silent farewell to Tommy Ruzzo. That ex-NYPD cop, former Precious Acres security guard, and one-time almost hitman was gone forever.

Tommy Aurora had officially taken his place. It even said so on his brand new passport. He found it amazing what money could buy. *Especially if you aren't too concerned about breaking the law.*

ACKNOWLEDGEMENTS

Thanks to my wife Heather and our beautiful kids. And to my trusted beta readers, Scott Ross and Paul Covington. A special thanks to my talented editor Elaine Ash, and my incredible lawyer, Kim Thigpen. And to Eric Campbell, Lance Wright, Rebecca T. Crowley and the team at Down & Out Books—thanks for bringing Tommy & Shayna into the world.

S.W. LAUDEN is the author of the Tommy & Shayna capers, including *Crosswise* and *Crossed Bones*. He also writes the Greg Salem mystery series, including *Bad Citizen Corporation*, *Grizzly Season*, and *Hang Time*. His short fiction has been published by Shotgun Honey, Out of the Gutter, Akashic Books, Short Stack Books and Crimespree Magazine. He lives in Los Angeles.

http://swlauden.com/

OTHER TITLES FROM DOWN AND OUT BOOKS

See www.DownAndOutBooks.com for complete list

By Jerry Kennealy
Screen Test
Polo's Long Shot (*)

By Dana King
Grind Joint
Resurrection Mall (*)

By Klavan, O'Mara, & Salzberg
Triple Shot

By S.W. Lauden
Crosswise
Crossed Bones (*)

By Paul D. Marks and
Andrew McAleer (editor)
Coast to Coast vol. 1
Coast to Coast vol. 2

By Gerald O'Connor
The Origins of Benjamin
Hackett

By Gary Phillips
Treacherous
3 the Hard Way

By Thomas Pluck
Bad Boy Boogie (*)

By Tom Pitts
Hustle
American Static (*)

By Robert J. Randisi
Upon My Soul
Souls of the Dead
Envy the Dead

By Charles Salzberg
Devil in the Hole
Swann's Last Song
Swann Dives In
Swann's Way Out

By Scott Loring Sanders
Shooting Creek and Other
Stories

By Ryan Sayles
The Subtle Art of Brutality
Warpath
Let Me Put My Stories In You (*)

By John Shepphird
The Shill
Kill the Shill
Beware the Shill

By James R. Tuck (editor)
Mama Tried vol. 1
Mama Tried vol. 2 (*)

By Lono Waiwaiole
Wiley's Refrain
Dark Paradise
Leon's Legacy (*)

(*)—Coming Soon

Proof

Made in the USA
Charleston, SC
17 February 2017